I0724616

Realms Of The Fae 6
Woven From Dreams

Realms Of The Fae 6
Woven From Dreams

Avril Sabine

Cracked Acorn Productions
Australia

Realms Of The Fae 6: Woven From Dreams

Published by

Cracked Acorn Productions

PO Box 1365

Gympie, Queensland 4570

Australia

978-1-925941-39-5 (Ebook)

978-1-925941-40-1 (Print)

Genre: Young Adult Urban Fantasy

Copyright 2021 © Avril Sabine

Cover design by Cracked Acorn Productions

All rights reserved

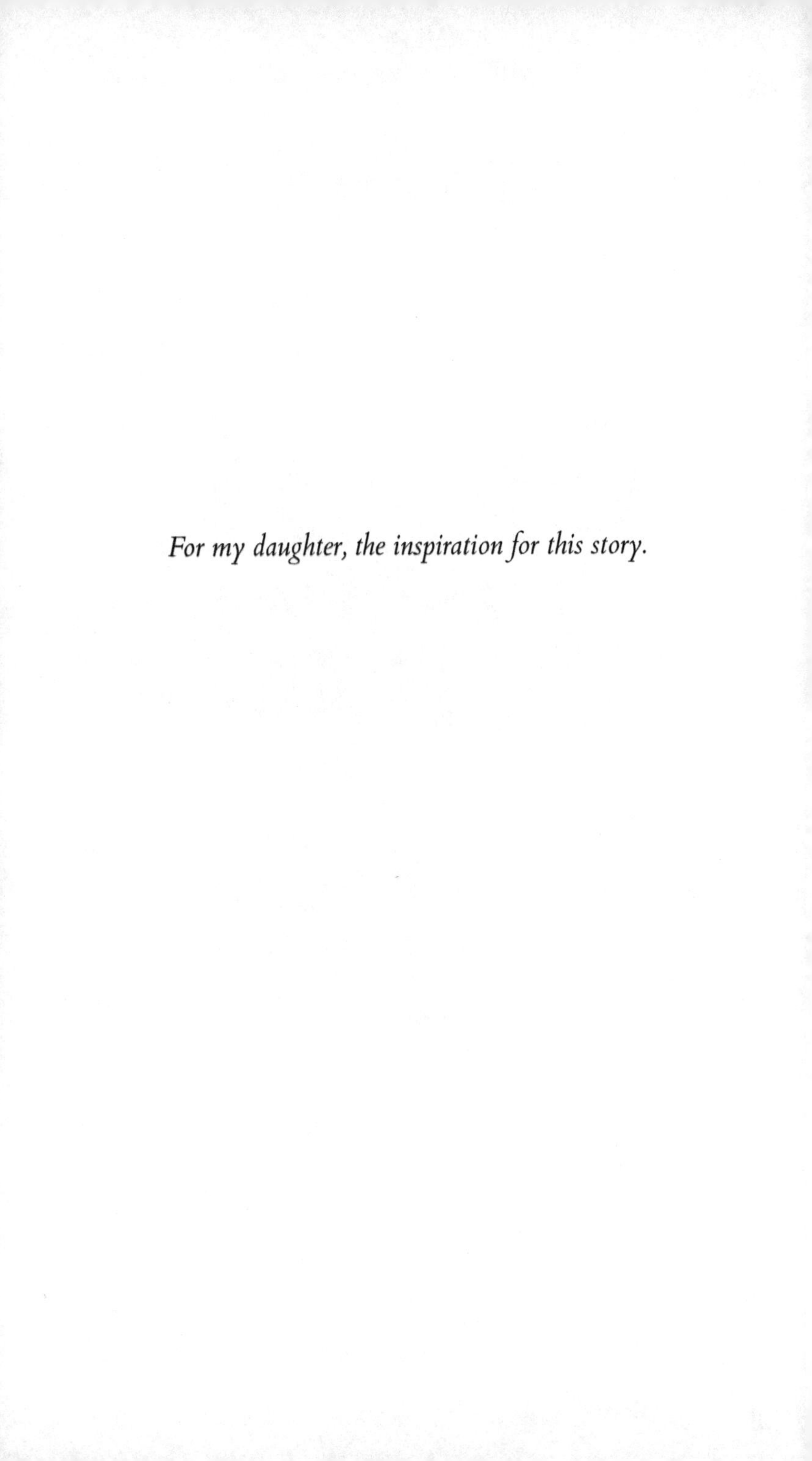

For my daughter, the inspiration for this story.

Elsie has been losing things in her sleep for as long as she can remember. Things she doesn't really want. Everyone has always told her she must lose them some other way. That no one loses things in their sleep. But when her boyfriend disappears, after she falls asleep next to him, she needs to figure out what's going on. And discover who the green eyed Fae is that she sees in her dreams. The one who keeps telling her she's dreaming.

*

This story was written by an Australian author using Australian spelling.

Chapter One

Elsie struggled to keep her eyes open, aware of Jaxson lying on the lounge room floor beside her, cushions from the couch beneath their heads. She kept her gaze firmly on the television screen, having no idea what had happened in the movie. Had Jaxson moved closer to her? Why couldn't she find the words to break things off? Marinda had said two more weeks wouldn't hurt. To finish things at the end of the June-July school holidays. She couldn't last that long. The previous night was a perfect example of why.

Jaxson's mum had twenty acres with an old caravan on it, north west of Brisbane, which she and her sister had inherited when their father had passed away the previous year. Neither of them could decide what to do with it, so it sat there, empty. The perfect place for parties during school holidays. No neighbours to complain and no parents to keep an eye on what they were up to. Which had been a problem since Jaxson had wanted to be up to a little bit more than she'd been interested in. Not that he'd pressured her or anything. She'd just hated to destroy the hopeful expression he'd had. It seemed to be a habit of hers lately when it came to him and she always felt so terrible that she couldn't feel for him the way he obviously felt for her. Yet she also didn't want to hurt him when she ended things and she had no idea how to go about that.

She felt a light tug on her hair. She didn't need to turn her head to know he was wrapping the long, dark blond strands around one of his fingers. He did it so often, fascinated by her hair that was a couple of shades darker than his own closely cropped hair.

She allowed her eyes to close, wondering if ignoring him would work. The gentle tugging continued. She let a silent sigh escape. After the movie. No matter how difficult it would be, she would end things with him after the movie. It wasn't fair to either of them to let things continue as they were. It felt like her life was on hold while she waited for the right moment and the correct words to end things between them. Words that wouldn't hurt him. She was beginning to think they didn't exist.

Keeping her eyes closed, she tried to think of an opening sentence. What did you say to someone when there was nothing really wrong with them other than they bored you? The old 'it's not you, it's me' was overdone. No one believed that line these days. So what could she say? He was nice. Although sometimes he was a little too nice to people who didn't deserve it. Friendly. Which could be a bad thing when you were in a hurry and his many friends kept waylaying him. He had a good sense of humour and certainly more than his fair share of looks. About her only complaint was the stupid way his mum had spelt his name. Another sigh escaped, this one a little louder than the first. She stilled when his fingers stopped tugging on the strands of her hair.

Had he heard her sigh? She remained perfectly still, her breathing slow and steady. Tiredness tugged at her and she tried to open her eyes. A young man leaned over her. It took her a few seconds to realise she was dreaming, her surroundings out of focus, her gaze fixed on the young man. His long black hair was drawn back from his face to show the tips of his ears were pointed, his green eyes startlingly vivid. He was too beautiful to be anything other than a dream. She wanted to reach up and touch him, run her fingers across his narrow face. But that would make the dream vanish. And she didn't want that. Now why couldn't she find someone like him in real life? Without the pointed ears, of course.

She blinked and in that fraction of a second, the dream vanished and she was lying in front of the television, staring at the menu screen, disappointment washing over her. The opening music was on its short loop and she wasn't sure how she'd fallen asleep when she'd been determined to remain awake. A smile slowly formed. Not that she was complaining after having had a dream like that.

She rolled to the side, expecting to find Jaxson lying beside her. Her half formed smile faded. She was alone, with only the many cushions from the couch scattered across the cream coloured carpet. Sitting up, she glanced around the lounge room. No one. She half reclined so she could get her phone from the pocket of her jeans. She checked the time. One in the afternoon. Her stomach grumbled, highlighting the fact she'd missed lunch and it had been hours since breakfast. Maybe that was what he was doing. He was probably hungry, too. It'd be just like him to make something for the two of them to eat.

Stumbling to her feet, she smothered a yawn as she headed for the kitchen. Remaining in the doorway, she scanned the room. It was exactly the way she and her mum had left it after breakfast. Dishes in the draining rack, now dry, the curtain at the window over the sink was half drawn open and the tablecloth remained on the round, four seater table in the corner. Annoyance arrowed through her. Had he left without saying goodbye? That didn't seem like him at all.

Taking out her phone again, she checked her messages. There were several from Marinda, a couple from other friends, but none from Jaxson. Returning her phone to a pocket of her jeans, she searched the rest of the house, finishing up in the lounge room. Anger rushed in on her. He'd walked out on her while she'd been asleep. After all the worrying she'd done over sparing his feelings, he'd gone and done that to her. Taking out her phone, she sent him a message.

I wouldn't have thought you'd be so rude as to leave without saying goodbye. We're ⱥnished.

She slid her phone back into her pocket, pushing aside the guilt that tried to form now the initial rush of anger was fading. She tried to focus on something else rather than think about what she'd done. It wasn't like she was the one who'd walked out on him with no word. Thoughts of Marinda came to mind, but they only had her circling back to Jaxson. Marinda would have to get over the breakup. Or date Jaxson herself. Taking her phone out once more, she sent a message letting her best friend know her and Jaxson were over and she could date him if it was that big a problem. She grinned at the reply.

ſ s imI'd never do that to you.

I don't hate hiH. ſ nd it wouldn't bother He. j e ꝶst bores He.

She settled in at the kitchen table, sending messages back and forth to her friend, regularly smiling and a few times laughing aloud.

She continued messaging Marinda as evening fell and she prepared dinner. Her mum was away for work this weekend. Some conference her boss had demanded she attend, even though she'd tried to get out of it. Elsie leaned her hip against the kitchen bench, a fork held above the rump steak sizzling in the pan as she waited to flip it. This was her last year of school and she had no idea what she was going to do once she finished. Whatever it was, she wasn't going to end up in some boring job like her mum, doing things she hated all the time. Being ordered around and stuck with the most tedious of jobs all so her boss could keep the fun parts of the work for himself.

After dinner, having planned to get her assignments finished this first weekend of the school holidays, she headed for her room. She'd barely stepped inside when her phone rang. Not recognising the number, she almost let it go to her message bank. "Hello?"

"Elsie? This is Jaxson's mum. Is he there? I'm guessing his phone is flat since all my calls go straight to his message bank."

"Hi, Mrs Bryant. He took off sometime after I fell asleep watching a movie. Without saying goodbye."

There was a moment of silence before Mrs Bryant spoke again. "Are you certain? That doesn't sound like him."

Elsie hesitated. "Yes." When the silence stretched out, she spoke again. "Maybe?"

"Do you know where he might have gone?"

"I thought he went home."

"Are you certain?"

Elsie automatically nodded. "Yes."

"If you hear from him, can you tell him to call me? I'm worried."

"Sure."

"Thank you, Elsie."

The line went dead and Elsie stared at her phone. Where had Jaxson gone? She tried to think of all the possibilities. There were none. He might be sociable and like having camp outs at the caravan, but he always let his mum know where he was going and when he'd be home. Always. A shiver ran down her spine and she tried not to think about what might have happened. His house was five streets away from hers. She'd thought the neighbourhood was quiet. What if she was wrong?

Slipping her phone into her pocket, she checked all the doors and windows were locked before she returned to her room. Focusing was difficult and progress on her assignments was slow. She couldn't stop wondering what had happened to Jaxson on his way home. Had a friend had an emergency and called him for help? It was the only explanation she could come up with. She again pushed aside the guilt and instead tried to focus on her assignments.

Jaxson was still missing on Monday and the police finally took it seriously. Elsie sat in the car beside her mum, who'd taken the morning off work to be with her while the police had interviewed her. She stared out the window, the car heater on full, trying not to think about all the questions that had been fired at her. She hadn't been able to tell them any more than she'd been able to tell Mrs Bryant.

She stared unseeing out the window. It seemed surreal. She rubbed her wrist where she'd once worn a gold bracelet with tiny diamond chips scattered across it, her hand slipping beneath the sleeve of her knitted jumper. The bracelet had been a gift on her fifteenth birthday from her great aunt Elsie, the woman who'd delivered her when her mum had gone into labour early. She'd woken one morning, unable to find the bracelet, and Great Aunt Elsie's words came back to haunt her. 'One day you'll lose something even more valuable if you don't take better care of your things.' It had been the first and last expensive gift her great aunt had given her. The last two birthdays she'd given her gift vouchers. She missed the unique gifts from her great aunt. Although how expensive the bracelet had been had made her uncomfortable. A shiver ran down her spine. Jaxson had vanished as completely as the bracelet. She hoped that unlike the bracelet, he'd be found.

"Maybe you should stay with your father these holidays," Brenda said.

Elsie half jumped at her mum's unexpected words. She finally looked away from the passing scenery. "Didn't you say last week that I didn't have one?" A smile fleetingly formed at the memory.

"That was when I was waiting for him to pay child support. He was late again."

Elsie studied her mum, surprised at how tired and drawn she looked. "Are you okay?"

"Work is busy. My boss is cutting back on his hours so he can spend more time with his family, which means more responsibility for me."

"That'll be good, won't it?"

Brenda shrugged. "We'll have to wait and see. I can't see it lasting long." She glanced over at Elsie. "You never answered me about staying with your father."

"I didn't think it deserved an answer. Seriously, Mum. He's not responsible enough to pay child support on time. Do you think he'd be responsible enough to look out for me?"

"Lock all the doors and windows and don't go anywhere alone. Better yet, don't go anywhere at all."

"Mum." She drew the word out. "I'm not about to sit in a locked house the entire holidays." She held up her hand when her mum started to speak. "But I also have no plans to go anywhere alone. I'm not an idiot."

Brenda sighed heavily. "I know, it's just..." Her voice trailed off and she slowly shook her head. "I can imagine this happening in Brisbane's city centre, but not in our suburb. I would have thought it too close-knit a community for someone to have grabbed him off the streets. I can't believe not one single person saw him after he left our place."

Elsie's gaze was drawn to the tree edged roadside, some of the bare branches stretching out above them. She didn't bother mentioning that no one had actually seen him leave their house. Again Great Aunt Elsie's words came to mind and a shiver ran down her spine. 'One day you'll lose something even more valuable if you don't take better care of your things.' She closed her eyes, pushing thoughts of Jaxson and the bracelet aside. It was impossible. The words kept repeating in her mind, accompanied by images she didn't want to see. No wonder she'd struggled to sleep properly the past two nights.

"Will you be okay if I go back to work?"

Chapter Two

Elsie opened her eyes in time to see her mum pull up out the front of their house. She tried to ignore the feeling that washed over her at the thought of being home alone. "I'm fine." And she would be. Once she was inside and had checked everything was locked. She'd been doing that almost obsessively lately.

"Are you sure?"

Elsie met her mum's hazel eyes, the same colour as her own. A few times she'd wished she'd inherited the same colour blue as her father's eyes. "Go to work and stop worrying." She emphasised each of the words. "I'm not a little kid."

"Straight inside and lock the door."

She made herself roll her eyes. "Okay, Mum." She filled her tone with the usual exasperation she would have felt. "Stop fussing." Grabbing her handbag off the floor at her feet, she forced her lips into a smile before she opened the door. "I'll see you later." With a half wave over her shoulder, she shut the door as she was stepping away from it, keeping her gaze firmly on the front door rather than scan the area for danger. She shivered, trying to convince herself it was from the cold air. But it wasn't that bad with the sun out and her knitted jumper keeping her warm.

Surely whoever had taken Jaxson wasn't still in the area. Taking the key out of her handbag, she unlocked the front door, aware her mum remained parked on the side of the road. Slipping inside, she glanced at her mum, waving before she locked the door and leaned against it, her head tilted back so she stared at the white ceiling. How long would it take before she no longer felt uncomfortable in her neighbourhood? Or in her own home. No one had seen him leave the house. She couldn't get that thought out of her head. She'd been the last person to have seen him.

Pushing away from the door, she headed to her bedroom, hanging her handbag on the door handle and taking off her knitted jumper before she dropped onto the bed. She was so tired. Her sleep had been broken and she desperately needed more than a few minutes at a time. Not expecting she'd be able to sleep, she grabbed the book off her bedside cabinet and opened it up to the chapter she was halfway through. The story failed to hold her attention and she couldn't help wondering if she wanted to finish it. Her eyes grew heavy and it felt like she'd closed them for barely a moment before she was jerking upright, her heart racing and the room full of shadows, her dreams filled with vivid green eyes.

Switching on her bedside lamp, she leaned over the edge of the bed to pick up the book she'd dropped. Only her knitted jumper was on the floor. She leaned further over the edge, running her hand along the carpeted floor under the bed. When she still couldn't find the book, she staggered out of bed and dropped onto the floor, peering under it.

Frowning, she leaned forward more. There was nothing. Drawing back, she stood up and straightened the quilt, running her hands over the bed as she tried to find the book. It was nowhere. She scanned the room. Nothing was out of place. Only the book was missing. Again, she scanned the room. What had she done with it? As far as she knew, she didn't sleepwalk. Although she supposed anything was possible when she wasn't getting much sleep.

A message came through on her phone and she checked. It was Marinda asking if she could spend the night, that she didn't want to be on her own. Or put up with her mum hovering.

Of course you can. You're welcome to stay here as often as you like.

Marinda's reply came through almost immediately. *I'll be there in a couple of minutes.*

See you then. She sent the message, then had one last look for the book before checking all the windows were still locked. Satisfied they were, she headed towards the front door, waiting for her friend to arrive.

Minutes later a dark-coloured sedan pulled up out the front and Marinda clambered out, backing away as she talked to the driver, her hands moving to emphasise some of her words. She glanced over her shoulder several times, twice gesturing towards the house. Her black hair hung around her shoulders, drawn back from her face by a clip. She was a few metres from the car when she waved and spun to face the house, hurrying towards the door Elsie held open. She stopped and turned to watch the car drive off, glancing over her shoulder at Elsie. "You can't imagine how crazy Mum is driving me since Jaxson disappeared. You'd think I was going to disappear next."

Elsie stepped back out of the doorway. "I don't want to talk about it. Not after all the questions I had to answer this morning. I was starting to feel like I was a suspect." She spoke the words jokingly, but couldn't help wondering if there was some truth in them. She had been the last person to have seen him.

"How about we watch a movie or something." Marinda stepped inside, unbuttoning her jacket. "I've barely slept the last two days. Mum keeps checking on me all night as if expecting someone to steal me from my bed."

Elsie led the way to the television, putting on the movie she hadn't managed to watch with Jaxson. The menu music had her shivering as memories came back. She reached for the DVD player. "Did you want to do something else?"

"What's wrong?"

Elsie shook her head, lowering her hand rather than ejecting the movie and have to explain her thoughts. She didn't want to examine them, let alone explain them. Why had she sent him that message? She pushed the thought aside.

"Don't give me that," Marinda said. "What's wrong?"

She held her friend's gaze for a moment, seeing the determination in her eyes. Marinda would keep asking until she had an answer. "No one saw him leave here."

"He was kidnapped from your house?"

Elsie shrugged. "I don't know. No one seems to know anything."

"Were there signs of a struggle?" Marinda dropped onto the couch, her gaze remaining on Elsie.

Joining Marinda on the couch, Elsie sat sideways so she could face her friend. "I don't even know what that'd look like." She picked up the remote. "We watching this?" She didn't want to listen to the endlessly looping music. What if someone had taken him from her house and if they had, why hadn't they taken her too?

Marinda nodded. "What is the last you remember about seeing him?"

That she'd been trying to find a way to ditch him. Keeping that thought to herself, she started the movie. "Are we going to watch this?" She gestured with the remote. She didn't want to spend the rest of the day talking about it. Not after spending all morning being grilled by the police. Or at least that had been the way it had felt.

"Sure, but that doesn't mean I can't talk."

"I really don't want to talk about it." She kept her gaze on the movie, determined to focus this time. Or at least determined not to think about unsettling facts. What had happened to Jaxson? Was he still alive? Images of a shadowy figure digging a long, shallow ditch in the middle of the bush filled her mind. She forced them aside. He had to be alive. She didn't hate him. Had only wanted to stop dating him. He was too nice a person to hate. She almost groaned at how ridiculous that thought sounded to her.

Marinda turned her attention to the television screen. "You will have to talk about it, eventually."

Not if she could help it. Yet again, she kept her thoughts to herself. She tried to focus on the movie, but all she could see were cushions scattered across the floor and Jaxson lying beside her, interspersed with images of a figure digging a hole. If she never saw the cushions again, she wouldn't mind in the least. She closed her eyes in an effort to block out the images. Leaning back onto the cushion behind her, she ended up falling asleep. Annoyed with herself at falling asleep again, she forced her eyes open.

Vivid green eyes filled her view and fingers lightly brushed across her face so she was forced to close her eyes. The air was filled with a peppery citrus scent. Before she could open her eyes again, a scream pierced her sleep, dragging her upright.

Marinda stood in the doorway, a finger pointed at her. "You vanished."

Elsie frowned, trying to make sense of Marinda's words, rubbing at her eyes in an effort to wake properly. "Vanished?"

Marinda nodded, lowering her hand. "You weren't there for at least four seconds. Maybe longer."

"Vanished."

"Will you stop saying that?" Marinda demanded. "And tell me what's going on. Where did you go?"

Elsie smothered a yawn with her hand, leaning back and expecting to sink into the cushion. She encountered the frame of the couch. Sitting up straight, she turned at an angle to stare at the spot where the cushion had been. "Where is it?"

"What?" Marinda remained in the doorway.

"The cushion." Elsie's gaze was drawn to the armchairs. Both of them still had their cushions. "The back cushion for the couch." She glanced at where her friend had been sitting earlier, finding the second back cushion remained in place.

"Forget about the cushion," Miranda said. "You vanished. Completely and utterly vanished."

"Impossible." Elsie scanned the room. "The cushion has to be here somewhere."

Marinda's eyes widened, her voice becoming hushed. "Do you think it was aliens? What if that was what happened to Jaxson? What if it's your house? This could be like some sort of Bermuda Triangle for aliens."

"It's not my house and Jaxson wasn't taken by aliens." She rose far enough off the couch to peer over the back of it. The floor was clear. "What happened to the cushion?" She took a deep breath at the slightly hysterical note in her voice. Aliens didn't exist. No matter how much Marinda wanted to believe in such things, they weren't real.

"Forget the cushion. What happened to you?" Marinda demanded.

"Nothing. I was asleep."

Marinda studied her. "You can't have been. You vanished. I know what I saw." She paused a moment. "Or didn't see. I knew there was more to life than everyone says there is. Now I have proof."

"Will you stop going on about it? I didn't go anywhere." Elsie rose from the couch. Surely she'd know if she'd left the house. She did a slow circle as she tried to find the cushion. "What did you do with it?"

"Nothing." Marinda took a step into the room. "I'll prove it. Next time you sleep, we're going to record you."

Elsie held up a hand, taking a step back and stumbling against the couch. "No way. That's not going to happen."

Marinda grinned. "We'll see."

"No, we won't." Elsie glared at her friend. "You are not going to record me while I'm sleeping."

Marinda's grin remained in place. "I made dinner while you were busy vanishing."

"Did you hear me? You're not going to record me." She followed Marinda to the kitchen when her friend didn't answer. "Well?"

"Sorry, think I'm going deaf." Marinda gestured to the table, where there were two plates with steak and chips. "Not fancy, but I don't do meals that need heaps of prep."

"You and me both." Elsie pulled out a chair, remaining standing. "I'm serious and you can stop changing the topic."

Laughing, Marinda sat at the table. "Eat your food before it's cold. Or next time I'll let you starve."

Elsie dropped onto the chair, sighing. "Thanks for cooking."

"You looked wrecked and I was hungry."

Elsie thought of and discarded several comments, remaining silent as she ate the food. It wasn't like she could argue the comment. She always looked terrible when she didn't get enough sleep. Dark shadows under her hazel eyes, her skin unnaturally pale, an inability to concentrate and a tendency to appear startled when she did notice what was going on around her. Not a good look at all.

Chapter Three

After the meal, Elsie and Marinda silently cleaned up the kitchen together, the two of them in Elsie's room talking when her mum came home, checking on them. They both decided to have an early night, Elsie warning Marinda not to record her as she set up a mattress on the floor for her friend.

Marinda grinned, not replying even when Elsie warned her once again to not even think about it.

Sighing, Elsie tried to get comfortable, tossing and turning as she attempted to sleep. At once stage she became tangled in the sheet and she was tempted to throw the bed linen off or even push it onto the floor.

She woke to a torch shining in her face and Marinda gripping her shoulder as she shook her awake. She brushed the torch aside, squinting up at her friend. "What's wrong?" She kept her voice low, not wanting to wake her mum, struggling to remember her dreams. Had it been the guy with the vivid green eyes or had the figure standing over her been someone else? She couldn't remember. It was too hazy.

"You have to see this." Marinda also whispered, sitting beside Elsie on the bed once she sat up.

"See what?" Elsie rubbed at her eyes, reaching for her phone to check the time. She froze when she saw the screen of Marinda's phone she held up, her fingers centimetres from her own phone. "I told you not to record me."

"Keep watching. I took it forward to just before the spot you need to see." Marinda raised her other hand to point at the phone. "There. See. You vanished."

Fear exploded through Elsie and she wanted to turn the phone off. Or delete the footage. She did neither, taking the phone from Marinda and rewinding it. She watched the same few seconds over and over. "It has to be a trick. What did you do?"

"Nothing. I seriously did nothing. It's something you did. Or the aliens."

Elsie couldn't take her gaze off the screen. "There are no such things as aliens." It struck her that she wasn't all that had vanished. Her sheet had too, but it hadn't returned. She dragged her gaze from the phone to check that only her doonah was on top of her. The sheet was no longer between her and the doonah.

"If it isn't aliens, how do you explain that?" Marinda gestured towards the phone.

"I don't know, but there has to be a logical explanation." She returned the phone to Marinda, taking hers from the bedside cabinet where she'd left it. "There has to be a logical explanation." For both her and the sheet. She searched several phrases online, each relating to vanishing while sleeping. There was nothing. Or at least nothing sane. She used different terms to search the topic in the hope she'd find something that actually made sense. Disappearing, not existing, dematerialise, become invisible and several others.

Marinda looked up from her phone. "This guy stayed awake for eleven days. Maybe you shouldn't go to sleep again until we know what's happening to you. What if eventually you don't come back?"

Elsie closed all the web pages she had open. "There's nothing wrong with me and nothing happened. It's probably a glitch in your phone or something. It might have overheated." But that didn't explain the missing sheet. She shied away from that thought.

Marinda gave her a disbelieving look. "Sure. Right." Her tone matched the look.

"I'm not going without sleep." It had been bad enough the past couple of days not sleeping properly. There was no way she could deliberately skip sleep completely.

Marinda scrolled down the page she was looking at on her phone. "What about this?" She tilted the phone. "Lucid dreaming. It might help you figure out what's going on."

Elsie took Marinda's phone and read the article before handing it back. "You think I'm going to learn how to do that in the minutes before I return to sleep?"

"You're not going to sleep." Marinda took her phone back. "Not until we figure out what's going on. I'm not going to have you disappear, too. Completely disappear and not come back."

Elsie slipped an arm around her friend's shoulders. "Quit worrying. I'm not going anywhere." She couldn't stop thinking about Jaxson. Had he thought the same?

Marinda leaned her head against Elsie's. "You better not."

"Well, actually, I am going somewhere." She tried not to smile, but it was difficult.

Marinda drew back to meet her gaze. "Where?"

"To sleep." She let the grin escape, laughing when Marinda glared at her, shoving her lightly.

"That's so mean."

Elsie sobered. The sheet was probably at the bottom of her bed from how she'd tossed all night. She'd find it there in the morning when she looked. "You have nothing to worry about."

Marinda sighed heavily. "I better not."

Elsie stretched out in the bed, drawing the doonah up, grateful her mum liked to have the heater on all winter. Not that Brisbane became that cold compared to other places, but it was more than cold enough for her. "Go back to sleep."

Marinda remained sitting on the edge of the bed, watching Elsie.

She peered up at her friend. "You can't seriously think I'm going to be able to sleep while you're staring at me like that. It's creepy."

"Good. I don't want you to sleep." Marinda's mouth dropped open and she breathed in sharply.

"What's wrong now?" Elsie wanted to close her eyes and go back to sleep. She was tired. Stifling a yawn, she slowly shook her head, unable to move it much while resting it on her pillow. "Actually, I probably don't want to know. Not if it'll make it difficult for me to sleep."

"What if it's you?"

"What do you mean?"

"You lose things in your sleep. That bracelet from your aunt, that awful scratchy blanket we both hated, the cushion from the couch and Jaxson."

She didn't mention the sheet. "I do not. I probably sleepwalk and put them somewhere." She just hadn't figured out where yet. Obviously, she was good at hiding things in her sleep.

"Let's test it." Marinda hurried over to the set of drawers that was covered in makeup, hair ties, trinket containers and jewellery. "What about this?" She held up a hair clip shaped like a butterfly.

"If your theory is right, why would you give me something I like? Something we both like?" She started to tell Marinda to bring the hair clip over anyway. Anything to get some sleep. Marinda spoke before she could.

"What don't you like then? There has to be something you wouldn't mind losing."

"Just bring the clip over."

"No. You're right. We both like it and how could I borrow it if you lose it in your sleep?"

"Fine." She spoke the word through gritted teeth, trying to think of something so she could get the conversation over with and go back to sleep. It was the first time she'd been able to sleep properly since Jaxson had disappeared and she could only think it was because she wasn't alone with her thoughts. Marinda was in the room too, her soft breathing letting her know she wasn't alone. Or at least it had when they'd both decided to sleep. "Why are you awake, anyway?"

"I don't know. Something woke me." Marinda made a dismissive gesture. "Forget about that. It's not important. What don't you want to keep?"

"The ugly cat ornament Dad gave me for my thirteenth birthday. The one that looks like it might be possessed. Or constipated."

Marinda laughed. "I never would have thought there was such a thing as an ugly cat ornament. Especially since there's no such thing as an ugly cat. Where did you put it?"

"Bottom drawer." She pointed towards the set of drawers the hair clip was on.

It took Marinda nearly a minute to find it. She held it up triumphantly. "Why do you need to keep so much junk?"

"It's not junk."

Marinda glanced at the cat ornament she held.

"Okay, that's junk. But I can't exactly throw it out. What if he asked what I did with it?"

Marinda crossed the room and placed the ornament in Elsie's hand. "Tell him aliens took it."

The ceramic ornament felt cool in her hand. "Now can I sleep?"

"Sure." Marinda turned on the torch and turned off the bedside lamp. "Night."

Elsie looked up at Marinda, who remained by the bed. "I'm not about to sleep while you're hovering over me." She spoke again when Marinda took several steps back. "And don't record me."

"How are we going to know what happens otherwise?" Marinda asked.

"Just don't-" She broke off at the expression on her friend's face. She recognised the stubborn look. Rather than waste her breath, she rolled onto her side and pulled the doonah over her head.

"How can I record you if you do that?" Marinda asked.

Elsie smiled, closing her eyes and not bothering to answer. The ceramic had warmed and she loosened her grip on the ornament. She almost hoped it did disappear. It was the ugliest thing imaginable. Thoughts of it made her mind wander to her father and her mum's suggestion of staying with him. She was safe here and there was nothing wrong with her or the way she slept. Marinda just had an overactive imagination. She fell asleep thinking about lucid dreaming and wondering why anyone would want to direct their dreams. She preferred to see where they took her, like watching a movie or reading a book.

Hands drew the doonah away from her face.

She stared up at the young man she'd dreamt about the day Jaxson had disappeared. He leaned over her, clearly visible in the soft lighting. She opened her mouth to speak.

He pressed his fingers against her lips, preventing her from saying a word. Like before, his long black hair was drawn back from his face to show the tips of his pointed ears and his eyes were as vivid a green as she remembered. He leaned closer before he spoke. "Dreaming." His word was barely a whisper.

The warmth of his fingers against her lips had her wanting to protest. He felt too real to be a dream. Besides, she never repeated a dream. Someone she couldn't see from where she lay on a firm mattress distracted her from speaking.

"Caidon! How long does it take you to find the unwanted object and send the dream spinner on their way?"

Caidon drew back to glance over his shoulder, his fingers remaining against her lips. "It's not like it's always obvious what they've brought with them." He met her gaze and pressed his fingers a little harder against her lips before drawing them back and pulling the doonah down further.

She again started to speak, stopping when he gave a slight shake of his head and pursed his lips like he was shushing her. She frowned. What was wrong with speaking? And who was the person she couldn't see from where she lay on the mattress? Did they have pointed ears too?

Caidon took the ornament from her loose grip and again glanced over his shoulder. Then he leaned close enough his breath brushed against her cheek, before whispering in her ear, "Do you want the dream weaver to imprison you?" He pulled the doonah up as he drew back, covering her face.

Chapter Four

Elsie remained motionless, shock racing through her at Caidon's words, a peppery citrus scent filling her senses. She struggled against the doonah, sitting up in the darkness. It took her a few seconds for her eyes to adjust to the faint light coming through her window from a streetlight that was across the road and in front of the next house down. She was in her bed. And back in her room.

Marinda sat up, protesting when Elsie turned on the light. "What are you doing?"

Elsie stumbled out of bed, tripping on the doonah she was tangled in and sitting down hard on the edge of the bed. "Did you record me?" Untangling herself, she glanced up at her friend who crossed the room to pick up her phone.

"It happened again, didn't it?" Marinda stared at the screen. "You vanished again. What happened while you were gone? How did you know you vanished?"

Elsie patted the bed down, checked under it and then stripped the linen from it as she checked for the ornament.

"Why would anyone want such an ugly cat ornament?" She stared down at her mattress, all her linen on the floor beside her feet, the top sheet not amongst the pile.

Marinda stopped by her side to stare at the bed. "Did you see them?"

She stared unseeing at the mattress.

"Elsie!"

The sharpness of Marinda's tone drew her attention and she finally managed to focus on something other than the missing ornament. "What?"

"Did you see the aliens?"

"He had long black hair and pointed ears." She slowly shook her head. "It had to have been a dream. Like he said."

"Like who said?"

"Caidon."

Marinda dropped her phone onto the bare mattress and gripped her arms. "Elsie. Make sense. Who is Caidon? And who said what?"

"Caidon pressed his fingers against my lips and said I was dreaming." She raised her fingers to press them against her lips where his had been. "He felt real."

"What changed?"

"What?" She really wished Marinda would make sense.

Marinda shook her slightly. "Focus. What did you do different? Why did you see the aliens this time?"

She started to tell Marinda it hadn't been the first time when another thought occurred to her. "Do aliens have pointed ears? And his eyes were such a bright green. Like emeralds. I thought aliens were meant to be strange, ugly looking creatures."

"We don't know that for certain." Marinda shook her slightly again. "What did you do different this time?"

She stepped away from her friend, pulling out of her grip. "Will you stop doing that?"

"You shouldn't complain. I considered slapping you. Don't they do that for shock? Or is that only when people are screaming hysterically?"

Elsie took another step back, running into her bedside cabinet. She pointed a finger at Marinda. "Don't even think about it."

Marinda grinned. "Too late, I already have." Her grin faded. "Tell me exactly what happened. Every little bit."

She tried to make sense of it, thinking over all that had occurred. Starting slowly, her words soon came out in a rush as she became more certain of everything. "It really happened. I wasn't dreaming it. That ridiculous ornament is gone and I know the difference between a dream and reality."

"Why did he call you a dream spinner? What is that? And what is a dream weaver?" Marinda stared at her screen as she tapped her questions in to a search bar on a web browser. "And what sort of alien has pointy ears?" Her fingers stilled. "Huh."

Elsie moved closer so she could stare at the screen. "Fae."

"Is that what he looked like?"

Elsie nodded. "Yeah."

"Ooh. Much better than aliens. Can you take me with you next time?"

"Are you kidding? What if they take you like they took the cat ornament?" Her mouth opened, no sound coming out.

"Or took Jaxson."

Elsie nodded, Marinda's words echoing the ones in her head. "We have to get him back." Just because she didn't want to date him, didn't mean she wanted to leave him with the dream weaver. Especially since it looked like she was the cause of his disappearance. Like the police had thought.

"We don't even know that's what happened to him."

"I know." She was certain of it. Nothing else made sense. Not that her theory completely made sense. Fae shouldn't exist. Nor should the ability to travel to them while sleeping "What did you learn about dream weavers and spinners?" She gestured towards Marinda's phone.

"Dream weavers are a program or a song. Searching dream spinner didn't help. Or searching for them together." Marinda lowered her phone. "You can't go back. Caidon said the dream weaver would imprison you. What would I tell your mum? What would I tell mine? She'd be even more freaked than she currently is. She'd definitely expect me to go next."

"You want me to leave Jaxson there?"

"No, but…" Marinda's voice trailed off and she threw her arms around Elsie. "I don't want you to vanish so that I never see you again."

She returned her friend's hug. "What do you suggest?"

"Tell the police."

Elsie drew back so she could meet Marinda's gaze. "Are you crazy? They'd never believe us. We'd either be in trouble for playing a cruel joke or thought insane."

Marinda clung to her. "You can't go. Or if you do, you're taking me with you. Surely between the two of us we can get Jaxson and get out of there. Wherever 'there' is."

"We need to find out all we can about the Fae." She untangled Marinda's arms from her. "Are you going to help me research them?"

"Elsie-"

She interrupted her friend. "I'm going after him. As soon as I learn all I can about the Fae."

"You're insane."

She grinned. "Obviously. What sane person vanishes in their sleep to give things to the Fae?"

"Why would they want your unwanted things?"

She stared at Marinda, thinking of all the things she'd lost over the years. Even Jaxson. All of them unwanted in some way or other. "That's a good point. Why would they only want the things I don't want?"

"Oh," Marinda exclaimed.

"What?"

"You didn't want Jaxson. You wanted to get rid of him."

"You knew that," Elsie pointed out.

"Yes, but…" Marinda's voice trailed off and she made a gesture with her hand, frowning. "You…" Again her voice trailed off. Her frown cleared. "You wanted him as much as you wanted the cat ornament."

"I told you I was going to break things off. What did you think I meant when I said that?"

"That he wasn't exciting enough. You said he bored you."

"It wasn't because he wasn't exciting." She tried to think of how to explain it. "He was…" She sighed. "Does it really matter? He's gone and I need to get him back."

"It does matter. What if it's dangerous? Are you going to risk your life for someone who bores you?"

"Yes, because he's not a bad person. He's actually too nice a person." A grin formed. "I figured it out."

"Figured what out?"

"He makes me feel guilty all the time. He always does the right thing, even when it'd be so much easier to do something else. No matter if it's big or little."

"So if he was bad he wouldn't be so boring?" Marinda slowly shook her head. "I didn't think you were the sort to go after the bad boy."

"I'm not explaining this very well after all. I don't want someone who's bad. I want someone who's human."

"Jaxson is Fae?"

She nearly growled. "No. But he's too perfect all the time. And I'm nowhere near perfect. It's like hanging out with a saint. You always feel you can't measure up. Like all your choices are wrong. He doesn't even hit the snooze on his alarm in the morning. Who never does that? It's not natural."

Marinda slowly shook her head. "I think you're the one who's not natural."

"Maybe, but I like being me. I like the mess in my drawers, I like to sleep in and I like not doing my chores and homework until the last minute. It felt odd starting my assignments so early this time." She gestured towards the items scattered across the top of the set of drawers. "And he asked me if I needed help tidying that up."

"He wanted to change you?"

This time she did growl. "No. He'd never try to change me. He was trying to be helpful."

Marinda took a step back from her. "Don't bite my head off. You're the one not making sense. He's a nice guy. You said so yourself."

"He is. He's also inhumanly perfect. And I'm not." She held up a hand when Marinda started to speak again. "Fae. That's all we need to worry about right now. Researching the Fae." Obviously, there was no point trying to explain how she felt to Marinda. Her friend just couldn't understand what she meant. She interrupted Marinda when she started to speak again. "Fae. Research. I'm going with or without your help."

"With." Marinda tapped on the screen of her phone, her gaze meeting Elsie's. "Always with." She glanced at the bed. "But do you think we should make that first? Your mum will want to know what's going on if she sees it like that."

Elsie sighed. "Fine. Then we research the Fae."

They were still scouring the internet when the sun came up, sprawled on the mattress as they compared notes. Elsie looked up when there was a light tap on her door before it swung open.

Brenda looked from one to the other several times. "Have you slept at all?"

Elsie nodded, conscious of the various web pages open on her phone. She wanted to close them down, but worried that would draw her mum's attention to them.

"What are you doing?" Brenda asked.

Marinda briefly held up her phone. "Reading about fairies. Or Fae as they're sometimes called. They're so much more interesting than aliens."

Elsie was tempted to close her eyes and groan at Marinda's words

"Well. Yes. Okay." Brenda looked between the two of them again. "Did you want breakfast?"

Elsie said no at the same time as Marinda said yes. She minimised the pages on her phone. "Okay. Sure. Breakfast would be good." She supposed she had to eat sometime. It wouldn't be a simple thing going after Jaxson. She had to find a way to stay there longer than a few minutes so she could look for him.

Brenda's eyes narrowed. "What are the two of you planning?"

"To travel to wherever the Fae live so we can bring Jaxson back," Marinda said.

Chapter Five

Elsie was half tempted to elbow her friend. She glared at her instead. "That isn't funny."

"It makes sense. If it's not aliens, then it has to be the Fae."

"Marinda." Brenda's voice was soft. "You do understand that Jaxson would have been taken by a human."

"We don't know that," Marinda said. "Who knows what is really in this world? He could be okay. Stuck in some kind of fairy ring and unable to escape for a hundred years. He'll come back looking exactly the same as the day they took him and all the people he knew will be dead."

"With how long people live these days, a hundred years isn't as long as it used to be. There might still be one or two left alive who knew him." Brenda sighed heavily, shaking her head. "What I meant to say is that you need to talk to someone about how you feel, not make up…"

"Fairytales?" Elsie suggested.

Brenda opened her mouth several times before shaking her head once. "Breakfast will be ready soon. Don't take too long coming to the table."

Elsie waited until the door was closed and she could no longer hear her mum's footsteps before she spoke. "Are you crazy telling her that?"

Marinda grinned. "She didn't believe me. They never do."

"Yes, but…" Her voice trailed off and she sighed instead. There was no point. Marinda liked her strange theories of aliens and other unexplained things. "Okay. Breakfast."

Marinda led the way to the kitchen, Elsie stepping into the kitchen after her.

Swearing softly, Brenda looked over her shoulder towards Elsie, shifting to try and prevent her from seeing the kitchen bench. "Don't look, Elsie."

Marinda stepped back in front of Elsie, blocking her view. "There's blood. You really don't want to look."

Elsie went hot and light headed at the thought, her skin feeling prickly. She closed her eyes and breathed slowly through her mouth, trying to think of something else. Anything else. The emerald green eyes of the Fae came to mind. Caidon. If only he'd been human. With his narrow face, vivid eyes and long dark hair, he'd intrigued her. Although from what she'd read about the Fae, he could have been a few hundred years old and not a few years older than her like he'd appeared to be.

"You can look now," Brenda said. "All cleaned up and covered."

Elsie opened her eyes to find Marinda was still in front of her, with her back now to her. "How bad was it?"

Brenda brought two plates to the table. Both were filled with scrambled eggs, tomato slices and toast. "Not bad. I should have dried my hands before I cut up the tomatoes." She placed a plate in front of Marinda, who'd sat down.

Marinda peered at the tomato, shifting it around. "You didn't get any blood on it, did you?"

Brenda returned to the table with a third plate. "I threw those ones out."

Elsie remained where she was standing, still feeling light headed. "Can we not talk about it?" She doubted she'd be able to eat the tomato. Not because she was worried there might be blood on it, but because of the colour. It was too close to the bright red colour she could see in her mind.

"Are you joining us?" Brenda gestured towards the table.

Elsie gave a jerky nod and dropped onto the chair in front of her plate. She picked up a fork and shifted the tomato to the side, trying not to look at it.

Marinda grabbed the slices off Elsie's plate and, along with her own, put them on one side of the toast before folding the toast down on top, hiding them from view.

Elsie sent her friend a grateful smile.

Marinda grinned before taking a large bite of the sandwich.

Elsie toyed with her food, moving it around as she stared at the scrambled eggs, trying not to see images of blood. Somehow, she managed not to sigh. The last thing she needed was her mum hovering like Marinda's mum was. She tried to focus on eating instead of replaying old memories in her head. They came anyway.

She'd been eight-years-old and her father and two of his mates had been watching a movie and had opened a bottle of scotch, mismatched glasses sitting on the coffee table. A scene came on with a man juggling two knives and they'd all joked about how easy it was. Only her father had actually attempted the feat. There'd been blood everywhere and one of his mates had called an ambulance while the other had grabbed a towel. It had been soaked through in minutes. She'd stood there, mouth open, eyes wide. Silent while internally screaming. They'd praised her for being so calm. None of them had been there to talk her through the nightmares she'd had for years.

Her gaze was drawn to her mum, who watched her carefully. She forced her lips to curve into a smile before she ate more of her breakfast. Even though she'd been eight, her mum had held her while she'd returned to sleep, often staying with her all night during the ones when she'd woken more than once. But that had been nine years ago. She was long past nightmares. Or at least she hoped she was.

"So…" Marinda drew the word out. "What are we going to do today?"

Elsie kept her gaze on her food, not glancing at her mum like she was tempted to do. "No plans." Or at least no plans she wanted to share with her mum.

"You're not planning on going anywhere today?" Brenda asked.

Elsie kicked Marinda's foot when she opened her mouth to speak. "No plans. We might watch another movie."

"That reminds me." Brenda glanced in the direction of the lounge room. "What happened to the back cushion off the couch?"

"I was going to ask you the same." Elsie met her mum's gaze, trying not to think of Caidon and the dream weaver. Did he look the same as Caidon or was he something else? Some strange creature that lived off dreams.

"Oh, come on, Elsie. You're not a little kid anymore. You can't keep losing things all the time." Brenda gathered her and Marinda's empty plates after a glance at Elsie's half eaten meal. "And how could you have possibly lost something as big as the cushion?"

"I didn't lose it." She tried to use the tone she'd always used when protesting being blamed for missing things. "Why do you always think it's me losing things?"

"Might be the Fae," Marinda suggested. "They swap babies with changelings so who knows what else they might do."

Brenda gave Marinda a look that said she was clearly unimpressed with the suggestion before taking the plates to the sink.

"You never know," Marinda protested. "Anything is possible."

Brenda opened her mouth, closing it when she checked her phone. She gave a single shake of her head. "I don't have time for this." She stopped in the doorway, glancing over her shoulder. "Stay home."

Marinda picked a piece of scrambled egg off Elsie's plate, waiting until Brenda was out of hearing before she spoke. "We aren't really going to stay home, are we?" She popped the egg in her mouth.

Elsie shrugged, sliding the plate over to Marinda. "I don't know how to get back there."

"It's easy. Every time had one thing in common. You took something with you that you didn't want. All you have to do is that lucid dreaming thing again and hold on to something you don't want."

"I don't know enough about them." She also didn't know if what she'd learned was even remotely true. Some of it had been information out of novels. Surely none of it was accurate. The authors had probably made it all up. Although there had been one author who'd claimed the Fae had told her the stories she'd written. "I have no idea where to go to learn the truth about them."

"It's always best to go to the source." Marinda worked her way through Elsie's breakfast. "At least that's what my dad says and as a researcher, you'd think he'd know."

"That doesn't sound very safe at all."

"So you're going to leave Jaxson there now?" Marinda scraped up the last of the egg with the fork.

"No." Elsie closed her eyes, trying to think of what she could do. Nothing seemed like a good idea. She rubbed the bridge of her nose.

"Headache?"

Elsie opened her eyes when the sound of Marinda's voice came from across the room. "I didn't hear you move."

Marinda placed the dishes beside the sink, her back to Elsie. "Tired?" Marinda faced Elsie, leaning against the kitchen bench. "Want a sleep?" She grinned.

Elsie shook her head, then shrugged. She was tired, but she didn't know if she wanted sleep. Not if it meant she'd be taken to the dream weaver. The person who Caidon was certain would imprison her. What if he was right and she ended up in some sort of prison?

"Elsie?"

She focused on her friend's face, surprised at the worry she could see on it. She crossed the room in a rush, throwing her arms around Marinda. "It's going to be okay. We'll get him back then forget we ever found out about the Fae." That would be the safest option. She tried not to think about Caidon. Why would someone as interesting as the Fae be even the slightest bit interested in getting to know her?

Marinda returned Elsie's hug. "And what about you? What if you keep taking things to them?"

Elsie ignored the unsettling feeling that formed in her stomach and spread upwards, making her feel ill. "I've never seen the Fae before I took Jaxson to them." Not that it made her feel any better to think of that.

"So you're not going after him yet?"

Elsie closed her eyes again, once more trying to ignore how ill she felt. Without opening her eyes, she took a step away from Marinda. She had no idea what to say.

"Elsie, what-" Marinda broke off. "You look lovely, Brenda."

Elsie opened her eyes and turned to see her mum, almost groaning at the suspicious look she was giving Marinda. "What time will you be home?"

Brenda shrugged. "Late. Don't worry about dinner for me. I have to attend a work event this evening."

"That sounds like fun. Will it be at a restaurant?" Marinda stepped forward so she was partially obscuring Brenda's view of Elsie.

"Yes." Brenda tilted her head to see past Marinda. "Are you okay, Elsie?"

She nodded. "Should I say goodnight now? Or will you be home before I head to bed?"

Brenda sighed. "Are you sure you're okay?"

Chapter Six

Elsie stepped around Marinda, crossing the room to hug her mum. "I'm okay. I was just asking. I'm not annoyed you're working late or anything."

"Something is clearly bothering you." Brenda drew back after returning the hug, keeping her hands on Elsie's shoulders and needing to look slightly upwards to meet her gaze.

"My boyfriend is missing. Don't you think that should bother me?"

"Are you sure that's all it is?" Brenda persisted.

"Yes, Mum. Now go to work. This is what you've been waiting for. Getting the chance to take on more responsibility. You never know, he might actually enjoy cutting back at work and you'll get to keep all those extra responsibilities." Elsie stepped back out of her mum's grip, trying to make her smile as natural as possible.

"Call me if you need me. I don't care what it's for or when it is," Brenda said.

"I will." Elsie was half tempted to put her hands behind her back and cross her fingers like she'd done as a child. There was no way she'd drag her mum into this mess. Not that she knew exactly what was going on. The Fae shouldn't exist. They were fairytales for children, not something that stole unwanted items from sleeping humans. Not one story she'd read had said anything about dream spinners or weavers.

Brenda studied Elsie a moment longer before she nodded, kissed her cheek and glanced at Marinda with another nod. "I'll see the two of you in the morning."

Elsie stared at the empty doorway, her mum's words ringing in her mind. In the morning. She closed her eyes. She had approximately twenty-four hours without her mum wondering what she was doing. Twenty-four hours before anyone would miss her if she became trapped with Jaxson. Not that it'd help her any. No one would know where to find them or how to reach them. Except Marinda. And that wouldn't help. No one would believe her.

"Are we doing this?" Marinda came to stand beside Elsie. "Are we getting Jaxson back?"

"We won't have a better chance." Or at least she didn't think they would. How often was her mum likely to work so late? And she didn't know how long it'd take to rescue Jaxson. Or if she could even manage to rescue him.

"Do you have something to give them?" Marinda asked.

"Give who?"

"The Fae. Something you don't want." Marinda grinned. "Like the cat ornament."

"Oh." She'd been busy focusing on her mum and Jaxson. No wonder she hadn't been able to follow the conversation. "I don't know."

"Come on." Marinda grabbed hold of her arm, tugging her towards her bedroom. "Surely you've got something you no longer want. Something you want to get rid of."

It took half an hour and Marinda randomly holding up everything she spotted. She pressed the plastic bracelet into Elsie's hand, the bright yellow almost a fluoro colour. "Are you sure you weren't procrastinating? Some of those items I showed you looked like you should have got rid of them years ago."

The plastic felt cold in her hand, reminding her of the cat ornament. "I'm not tired. How am I meant to sleep when I'm not tired?"

Marinda peered into Elsie's face. "You've got bags under your eyes. Are you sure you're not tired?"

"I think I should know how I feel." She sighed softly at the irritation she heard in her voice. "Sorry."

Marinda patted her shoulder. "It's okay. How about I heat some milk for you?"

"Why?" She frowned, thinking over Marinda's words. They didn't make any more sense the second time.

"To make you sleepy. That's what they do in some books," Marinda explained.

"I'd rather have a scotch." She winced. Saying the name of the drink aloud brought back memories of blood after being reminded of it recently. "Actually, make that a tequila." Anything had to be better than a scotch.

Marinda continued to study her. "Are you sure you're okay? Your mum seemed to think you weren't."

"She was probably picking up on our plans."

"We didn't have any plans at that point. Are you sure you're okay?"

She wanted to snap that there was nothing wrong with her, but then Marinda would be certain there was something wrong. "What other ideas do you have for going to sleep?" She held her breath, hoping the question would be enough to distract her friend.

Marinda studied her a moment more before she spoke. "We could walk over to my place and take some of my mum's sleeping tablets for you."

She slowly let out her breath, shaking her head before she answered. "I need to be able to wake when I arrive. Next suggestion."

Marinda shrugged. "I'm all out of ideas." She took out her phone. "I'll see what I can find online."

Worried about what her friend might end up discovering and expect her to try in an effort to sleep, Elsie took out her phone too and had a search for the best ways to fall asleep. It took them another half an hour to come up with a plan, Marinda complaining that they were running out of time.

Elsie had a warm shower, coming out to find Marinda had turned out all the lights and drawn the curtains, plunging the house into shadows. Her phone was sitting on her bedside drawers, soft music playing. She slipped on her sneakers before getting into bed, leaving her feet hanging over the end of the bed when she pulled the doonah up. There was no way she was going to turn up barefoot in some strange place. She clutched the bracelet that had been left on her pillow.

She tried to fall asleep. It didn't work. She turned to her side, but it was as successful as lying on her back had been. She finished the playlist Marinda had put on for her and was partway through a second one when she drifted off to sleep, still clutching the bracelet. Her hand tightened around the plastic when she opened her eyes to meet Caidon's gaze.

He leaned in close. "Dreaming."

She kept her voice as low as his. "You said that last time."

"Then listen and stop being awake when you come here." He drew the doonah back, prying the bracelet from her hand. "It isn't safe."

She grabbed his hand as the same peppery citrus scent filled the air, clinging to him. "Did you take Jaxson from me?" She met his vivid green eyes.

"Anything you bring here, that you don't want, belongs to the dream weaver." He dragged his hand from her grip, shaking her off again when she once more grabbed hold of him. "Let go of me. You need to return home before he comes back. Do you want to be caught?"

"Who is the dream weaver? And why do things I don't want belong to him?" They were her things. She should be able to say who did and didn't get them if she didn't want them.

"Let go." He untwined one of her hands from him.

She grabbed hold of him with it again as he worked on her other hand. "Help me get Jaxson back. Please, Caidon."

"How do you know my name?"

"I heard the dream weaver call you by that name. What is his name?"

Caidon shrugged, still trying to untangle her hands from him. "If he ever had another name, he's never shared it with anyone here."

"Where are we?"

His hands stilled. "If I answer your questions, will you return home before he catches you?"

"Why are you worried about him catching me?"

"I shouldn't be. I should let you find out what happens to dream spinners who realise this isn't a dream."

"Then why are you worried?"

He glanced over his shoulder. "He's coming. Are you going to be sensible and return home?"

"Not without Jaxson."

"You didn't want him, anyway." He tried once more to remove her hands from him.

"I didn't want him left here either." She let go of Caidon and rolled off the firm mattress, landing on the floor in a half crouch.

"You're making a bad mistake." Caidon advanced on her.

"What is going on here?"

Elsie spun to face the man who'd entered the room. "You're human." Her gaze was fixed on his ears that were rounded rather than pointed, his short brown hair making it easy for her to see them. "You're also young." She'd expected some kind of old, wise man with a name like the dream weaver.

"Older than I look and far older than many." The dream weaver turned to Caidon. "Why is she walking around?"

"I was working on dealing with her when you came in," Caidon said.

"That better have included putting her in one of the cages," the dream weaver said.

At the dream weaver's threat, Elsie glanced around the room. There was only one exit. And the dream weaver was blocking it. Yet she couldn't stand here and wait to be caught.

"Do something now, Caidon," the dream weaver demanded.

Caidon advanced on Elsie.

She backed away from him, running into a wall. When he was within arm's reach, she darted around him. Her heart raced as she sprinted towards the doorway, still not sure how she'd get past the dream weaver.

Caidon tackled her, the force of his movement causing both of them to crash into the wall beside the doorway. He kept his body pressed against hers, his mouth close to her ear. "I warned you. No one escapes from him. The only way out is to offer him something of greater value. And I doubt you have anyone who'd be willing to do that for you."

She started to speak. His hand clamped over her mouth, preventing her from saying a word. She struggled against his grip.

His other arm went around her chest, pinning her arms to her sides as he drew her away from the wall. His arm tightened around her, his hand remaining in place across her mouth. "It would be easier on you if you didn't struggle."

She glared at the dream weaver as he stepped out of the way, letting Caidon drag her down the corridor. She tried to bite his hand, but he had it clamped too tightly against her. If he removed it, she'd soon tell him that there was no way she was going anywhere without a fight.

Caidon grunted when her foot connected with his leg, causing him to stumble. "You could have avoided this. I warned you."

She tried to shake her head. She could barely move it. And speaking was still impossible. All she could do was make unintelligible noises and struggle to escape.

Caidon stumbled, colliding with the wall. He pressed her against it, turning her enough that he could meet her gaze. "Enough. You had your chance to leave this place. Chances I never should have given you. Now accept the consequences. Understand?"

She met his green eyes, glaring at him. No, she didn't understand. And she didn't know how she would do it, but she was going to escape. Without his help, if necessary.

He shook her slightly. "Do you understand?" He loosened his grip on her mouth.

She had just enough room to either bite or speak. She was extremely tempted to do the first. "Let me go."

"Impossible. I have no choice other than to obey his command."

Chapter Seven

When Elsie would have spoken again, Caidon clamped his hand over her mouth, preventing her. She glared at him, once again making unintelligible noises.

He continued to meet her gaze. "I'm sorry I have to do this to you." He tightened his grip around her before drawing her away from the wall.

She continued to struggle as Caidon dragged her down the corridor and into a kitchen, a trapdoor open on the far side of the room, steps leading down to a long narrow room. It was filled with cages, five on either side. Only three were filled.

In the first cage on the left, a young woman came to her feet. She gripped the bars. "I changed my mind, Caidon. You can go to our father and tell him. Any plan he might have for me would be far better than spending another day in here."

Caidon stilled, his arms tightening around Elsie. "You should have spoken sooner. I've already made a deal with the dream weaver."

The young woman tugged at the bars. "You had no right."

"You gave me that right when you begged me to help you. When I tracked you down here and asked if our father knew where you were. You gave me no choice when you refused to let me involve him," Caidon said.

Elsie stilled, listening carefully. Hoping that somehow they'd let slip some information that'd be useful to her. She forced herself to relax, leaning back against the warmth of Caidon's chest.

"What deal did you strike?" the young woman demanded.

"That I work for him for a year and a day having only the day of the full moon of each month to myself and being his to command in all things. In exchange, he'll release you without taking from you any unprocessed magic. If I fail to live up to my end of the bargain, I'm his to command for a decade, to be in chains for that entire time with no day each month for myself," Caidon said.

"Are you trying to kill me?" The young woman tried to shake the bars. They didn't budge. "Caidon! I can't live that long without my tree."

"Didn't you hear me say the full moon of each month is mine to do with as I wish? Autumn, I can bring you leaves and some cuttings to tide you over until the next month." Caidon took a step towards his sister, his movement forcing Elsie to shuffle forward.

Elsie had so many questions she wanted to ask, but she knew neither of them would willingly tell her anything. Silence was her best hope of learning something useful. Something she might be able to turn to her advantage. Although so far nothing they'd said had been of any use. Interesting, but not helpful.

Autumn took a step back from the bars, letting them go and shaking her head as she backed further away. "No. You're not cutting my tree. You know how painful that is to me."

"Not as painful as dying."

Elsie was thoroughly confused. Nothing she'd read anywhere had mentioned the Fae needed trees to live. Some things had said they were drawn to nature, but that was as close as the information had come to saying they needed trees.

"You have to come up with another plan," Autumn stated.

"There is no other plan. This is it. You were the one who said you'd prefer anything other than me going to our father."

Autumn closed her eyes, lowering her head, her dark brown hair falling forward to partially obscure her face. She slowly shook her head. "Tell the dream weaver you've changed your mind. Tell him I don't agree with the terms." She raised her head, her vivid green eyes meeting

Caidon's. "You need to get me out of here now. I'm having the dream spinner's child. I can't stay here."

Caidon recoiled as if struck, his grip on Elsie loosening. "No. Are you mad? Our father would never accept a child that was part human. Never. He's likely to disown you."

It took a few seconds for Elsie to register that Caidon's grip was light enough she'd be able to escape from him. Autumn's words had confused her. Hadn't Caidon called her a dream spinner? There was no way she could get anyone pregnant.

Autumn pressed a hand to her stomach, backing further away from the bars and Caidon. "No one will harm my child."

Elsie looked in both directions. To the left was the exit, to the right were the rest of the cages, two of which had people huddling in the bottom of them. One had a ragged blanket covering them and the other was half naked and thin enough that his ribs were clearly visible and his trousers hung baggily on him. She didn't know whether to dart forward and drag the blanket off the hidden captive or run for the exit. It took her nearly a minute to decide. The entire time, Autumn and Caidon continued to argue.

Elsie broke free from Caidon, darting forward to drag the blanket from the other captive. It was a woman, this one as gaunt as the male. She looked up at Elsie, her blue eyes faded and unfocused, her silvery blond hair matted and dirty, very few strands showing her natural colour.

The woman stretched out a hand to Elsie. "End it. Please end it. I can't cope with any more."

Caidon, who'd broken off in mid-argument with his sister, grabbed hold of Elsie. "You can't help them. They'll be dead within days, the magic drained from them like all the items brought here by dream spinners."

The male captive raised his head, looking directly at Elsie. He frowned, squinting up at her. "Am I dreaming?"

Elsie's mouth dropped open as she recognised Jaxson's voice. She tried to say his name, but no words formed.

"Is it really you, Elsie?"

She could only nod, still unable to speak. If it hadn't been for his voice, she wouldn't have recognised him.

Jaxson tried to rise to his feet, grabbing hold of the bars to pull himself up. He managed to get as far as kneeling, leaning against the bars he clung to. "Have you come to take me home, Elsie?"

Caidon drew her back against him when she would have gone forward. "She's here to join you in a cage."

"No. Not you too," Jaxson protested. "He's going to kill all of us. You have to escape. Have to bring help."

Elsie still couldn't say anything, too dazed to struggle when Caidon pushed her into the cage one down from his sister. It wasn't until the door clanged shut and Caidon locked it, that she was able to move and speak. She threw herself at the bars, gripping hold of them. "Don't leave me in here." Panic rushed through her at the thought of dying. At the thought of all of them dying. "Please, Caidon."

"Think he's going to let you out when he won't let his own sister out?" Autumn demanded.

"Caidon." Elsie's gaze followed him as he returned up the stairs, not looking back at any of them. "Caidon!" She called his name as he disappeared through the trapdoor. She slowly shook her head, unable to believe she was locked in a cage. Hitting the bars with her open hands, she was tempted to call his name again. She doubted he'd pay any more attention than he had all the other times she'd called his name. Her gaze was drawn to Autumn, who also stared at the trapdoor. How could he have left his sister locked up down here?

"What do we do now?" Jaxson was slumped against the bars, sitting on the floor.

Autumn dropped onto the floor, her hand going protectively to her stomach. "Wait to die." She hung her head again. "I never thought he'd ever want to be rid of me. He said he didn't. My friends warned me about the risk of being with a dream spinner. Of sleeping beside one. He said he would always want me. That he couldn't imagine life without me. Yet when I told him of the child, the next night I ended up here."

"It might have been the child he didn't want," Jaxson suggested. "Just because you ended up here, doesn't mean it was you he wasn't interested in."

Elsie winced, trying not to think about how Jaxson must feel, knowing for certain she didn't want him. "I'm sorry." She met his gaze when he looked over at her. "I'm sorry you ended up here."

"I'm sorry I wasn't who you wanted. What did I do wrong?"

She was tempted to close her eyes rather than see the hurt in his. She forced herself to keep meeting his gaze, no matter how difficult it was. He deserved at least that much after what she'd done to him. "I'm sorry I ditched you in a text. I shouldn't have done that. But I suppose you haven't been able to read them yet."

Jaxson nodded, still leaning against the bars. "The messages came through, one and two at a time. We figured out that it was only when a dream spinner arrived that I could get any messages."

"We?" She wanted to ask Jaxson why he was so calm, but was afraid of what his answer might be.

Jaxson glanced at Autumn. "The two of us. She told me all about dream spinners and weavers and the Fae and Dryads."

"Oh." She studied Autumn, wondering if the young woman was a Dryad. The tree comment made much more sense if she was one. She glanced at the other woman, the one who'd begged to end it. She was again hidden by the blanket.

"You can get us out of here. You just have to dream it," Jaxson said.

"How?" She had no idea how any of this worked.

"It's not that simple. She has to dream it when another dream spinner arrives. That's the only way she'll return home. Hitch herself to their return," Autumn said. "That's all dream spinners are capable of. They can't use magic to travel places on their own. They're useless."

"There's a way out of here?" Elsie tried not to let her hopes rise, but excitement filled her at the thought of escaping.

"Can you sleep when you need to?" Autumn asked.

Elsie's hopes plummeted. "No."

"Then we keep you awake until you're desperate to fall asleep," Autumn said. "And we get out of these cages so we can hold onto you when you return home."

"We need keys." Elsie tilted her head back so she could see the lock in the door. "Unless one of you knows how to pick locks."

Autumn and Jaxson both shook their heads.

Elsie sighed, momentarily closing her eyes as she rested her forehead against a cold bar. "Then it's impossible. I can't get to either of you."

Jaxson stretched his arm out through the bars. "Can you reach me, Elsie?"

She tried, her shoulder pressed tight against the bars, her arm aching with how hard she reached out to him. "I'm sorry." She lowered her arm, still pressed against the bars. "The corridor's too wide. I'm so sorry." She should have broken up with him before things reached this point. Before she'd left him in some strange place where he waited to die. But how could she have known any of this existed?

"Please, Elsie. Don't give up." Jaxson continued to stretch his arm out to her. "I can't take many more days of this. You don't know what it's like. It feels like he's draining every bit of life from me as he draws the magic from me. The magic you left in me by bringing me here."

She stared at his outstretched hand, torn between apologising and arguing that she hadn't deliberately left him here.

"Can you feel it? Can you feel one of them coming?" Autumn asked.

Chapter Eight

Elsie started to disagree, nodding her head when she noticed what felt like a hum of energy in the air.

"If you're asleep, you can catch a lift back to your world with them," Autumn said. "Not that it'll help if you won't at least try to reach us."

Elsie started to argue that she'd tried, but the look on Autumn's face made her believe the young woman had already made up her mind about the situation. She closed her mouth, trying to figure out how to escape. There was no way she could fall asleep right now. "How often do they come here? And how do you know they're from my world?"

"Dream spinners are always human. And dream weavers are spinners that gained the ability to control spinners and take the magic generated from their dreams. From lost dreams," Autumn said.

There were more questions she wanted to ask, but there was one more pressing than any other. "Have they gone or did I just get used to the feel of their magic?"

"They've gone," Autumn said. "They never stay long. You need to learn how to fall asleep in seconds."

She wanted to protest Autumn's demands. How was she meant to do that? She struggled to sleep on a good day, often waking throughout the night. "Is there another way out of here?"

"Useless." Autumn filled the word with venom, turning her back on Elsie. "You're completely useless. We're all going to die."

She started to protest Autumn's statement, but again she decided that now probably wasn't the best time to convince the young woman of anything. "How do I learn to fall asleep fast enough to hitch a ride with another dream spinner? If I can get out of here, I can return to help the three of you escape."

"Oh, of course you'll come back." Autumn's tone was dry and full of disbelief, her back still to Elsie.

Jaxson spoke before Elsie could protest Autumn's words. "You can always rely on Elsie. No matter what."

She looked across the corridor to him, once more feeling like she should apologise. "I will come back for you." Her voice was low and she tried to make sure he knew she was serious. "For the three of you." It wouldn't be right to take him and not the other two.

"I know." He hesitated. "I was hurt at first, when I realised that only the things you don't want get left behind here. And people. But it didn't take me long to realise that it wasn't your fault. That you couldn't help the way you felt and I'd probably done something to change the way you felt about me. I'm sorry for whatever it was that I did."

"No. You didn't do anything. It was me." She winced at how the words sounded. They were as lame as she'd feared they'd be. "I know how that sounds, but it's true. It wasn't anything you did." She drew in a deep breath rather than continue rambling in an effort to make him understand. "I'm sorry." She had no idea what else to say. Her words seemed so inadequate.

"Help get us out of here. That's all I ask." Jaxson smiled, a touch of humour mixed with a wry expression. "Maybe we should have stuck to being friends."

A sharp pain arrowed through Elsie at his words. How could she have left him in this place? Even accidentally. He certainly didn't deserve the way she'd treated him. "We could go back to being friends." Her words were hesitant.

Jaxson held her gaze for a moment. "I hope so."

"While you pair have been gazing into each other's eyes," Autumn said, "another dream spinner has come and gone."

Elsie faced Autumn. "I didn't notice." She needed to figure out how all this worked. Quickly. Her mum would be in a panic if she wasn't home before her.

Autumn turned her back on Elsie again. "We'll never get out of here. Not with how little you know about your abilities."

"She will get us out of here," Jaxson protested.

While Autumn and Jaxson argued about her, Elsie retreated to the back of her cell, sitting down and leaning against the wall. She tilted her head back, closing her eyes as she tried to focus on her surroundings. It didn't help. When the next dream spinner arrived, she was too wide awake to figure out how to catch a lift back with them. Autumn and Jaxson's argument didn't help, nor did Autumn's continual negative comments about her lack of skills. It wasn't like she'd known anything about dream spinners and weavers before today.

She tried to tune the argument out, half drifting off in the part waking state she sometimes ended up in before falling asleep. It was a struggle to maintain that state. Sleep dragged at her, trying to pull her under. She felt the hum of energy build again at the arrival of a dream spinner. Energy flowed around her, making the hair on her arms rise. It continued to increase, the words Jaxson and Autumn spoke fading into the background to become white noise.

"What are you doing?"

The sound of Caidon's voice nearly dragged her out of her half waking state. She clung to it, feeling the energy around her change. A hand grabbed her shoulder, starting to shake her as she followed the energy of the dream spinner back to their world. Back to her world. She woke in her bedroom, Caidon's hand still on her shoulder, Marinda's shriek causing her to wince.

Caidon stumbled away from her. "I can't be here. I can't leave the dream weaver."

Worried he'd leave, Elsie threw herself at him, wrapping her arms around his waist. "No. You're not leaving until you teach me how to do this. I need to get Jaxson out of there." She needed to help all of them escape, but Jaxson was a priority.

"You need a dream weaver to teach you. Not me." Caidon tried to pull out of her grip.

She held tighter, refusing to let go. "I don't know any dream weavers. You're going to have to teach me."

"What is going on?" Marinda demanded.

Elsie looked up at Caidon, their bodies pressed close together, her arms struggling to hold him. "Please. You have to help me. I can't leave him there."

Caidon stilled. "You must let me return. Before the dream weaver realises I'm gone. You would trap both me and my sister if you don't."

"Will you promise to return and help me learn how to travel in my dreams if I do?"

Caidon slowly shook his head. "I can't."

"Can't what? Promise or help?"

"Will someone answer me?" Marinda looked from one to the other. "What is going on?" She pointed a finger at Caidon. "And who are you?"

Elsie continued to meet Caidon's gaze. She'd tell Marinda everything later. Right now, she had to convince Caidon to help her. "Please. I'll help your sister escape if you help me." He didn't have to know she'd help Autumn, regardless.

"I can't do anything to help you. I can't promise something I can't do as I can't speak a lie. Let me go. If you care anything for those other than yourself, you'd let me go. I'm bound by my promises."

"Then at least take me back with you. Show me the way so I can try and get Jaxson out of there." Elsie continued to hold on to him, the warmth of his body warming hers. "Please, Caidon."

"This is him?" Marinda asked. "The one from your dreams."

"Please." She let him go enough to take hold of his hand, hoping he didn't try to escape from her limited grip.

"It's madness to return. You'll only get yourself caught again," Caidon warned.

"A chance. That's all I ask for. A chance to rescue Jaxson."

"Elsie!" Marinda grabbed hold of Elsie's arm. "Tell me what's going on. Did you find Jaxson?"

Caidon tugged Elsie away from Marinda. "A chance. That's all I can offer you." The peppery citrus scent filled the air as a dark green leaf formed in his hand. He crushed it and the world shimmered and reformed around them, the faint light of dawn doing little to penetrate the darkness of the forest.

Elsie tightened her grip on his hand, staring at the building in front of them. A forest pressed in around the rough-cut stone building that didn't take up much more space on the ground than a cottage would. Yet it looked like it wanted to be a castle with its tower on one side and narrow windows scattered across the front of its three storey high walls. "Where are we?"

Caidon drew his hand out of her grip. "Where you wished to be. This is where the dream weaver lives."

She grabbed hold of his hand when he started for the arched timber door set in the tower section. "Where are the cages?"

"Stay on the ground floor. There's nothing on the upper two floors for you. Take a left when you leave the entrance room. It leads to the kitchen." He again drew out of her grip. "I kept my word. Now you keep yours and let me return to the dream weaver."

She clasped her hands together when she would have again reached for him. "Thank you."

He met her gaze. "I've done you no favour. You'll be trapped again before the day ends." He held her gaze a moment longer before he turned and strode inside, leaving the door open behind him.

She hesitated. The darkness inside the building seeming worse than that of the forest that pressed in around it.

What if Caidon was right? What if she was trapped again before the day ended? She tried to take a step forward. Her body wouldn't cooperate. She wanted to go home. Wanted to forget any of this had ever happened.

Caidon's vivid green eyes filled her mind and she wished she could believe his earlier word. Wished she could convince herself this was all a dream. Nightmare maybe, but certainly not just a dream. Not even close.

She closed her eyes, trying to make her mind blank. Other images replaced the one of Caidon. Those in the cages were quickly followed by ones of her father. Blood filled scenes crowded her mind and she drew in a shuddering breath. She'd been unable to help him. Unable to help herself for many years, caught in nightmare after nightmare. What made her think she could face a nightmare and save someone else? Not just one, but three people.

Her shoulders slumped. She was kidding herself if she thought she could manage this. She should find a place to curl up and sleep and return home with the next dream spinner before the dream weaver found her. She should-

Energy filled the air, interrupting her thoughts. Another dream spinner was coming. This was her way out of here. She could either run or try and save Jaxson, Autumn and the other woman. She might not have another chance.

Before she could think it through, she found herself heading for the door. Then she decided it was probably better not to think too hard on it or she might find herself remaining frozen out the front of the building until the dream weaver did find and capture her.

She peered inside, her eyes quickly adjusting to the dimness. No one was inside and she scurried across the room to the single door and peered into a corridor. She went left, hurrying along it, half expecting to be caught at any second. She glanced into the room, heading towards the end of the corridor when none of them were the kitchen she was looking for.

It was at the end of the corridor that seemed far larger than the building had appeared from outside. She didn't know if it was an illusion or it really was bigger inside than out, but she didn't have time to dwell on it. The energy was building and the dream spinner would soon be gone.

Chapter Nine

Elsie nearly threw herself down the stairs when she reached the trapdoor, stopping in front of Jaxson's cage where he struggled to rise. She wrapped her hand around his on the bars. "We have to get out of here." Holding onto him, drawing his hand away from the bars to drag his arm past them, she turned and tried to reach Autumn. "Take my hand."

Autumn's arms remained at her side. "You're wasting your time. He chained us when he saw you'd escaped."

"Please. Try anyway." Elsie's gaze briefly dropped to the chains around Autumn's ankles before meeting her gaze again. The Dryad's eyes reminded her of Caidon. "Please, Autumn. They'll be gone soon."

Autumn pressed herself against the bars, the tips of her fingers lightly brushing Elsie's. "You'll soon see how impossible this is."

Recalling the state she'd been in before, Elsie focused on achieving the part waking sensation, breathing out slowly as her surroundings faded into the background. The energy was her focus and she tried to follow it to the dream spinner's world. Something tugged on her, not letting her go. She fought against it, but it was like heavy chains wrapped around her limbs, keeping her bound to where she stood. The energy faded and Elsie let go of Jaxson, her arms dropping to her sides, exhaustion washing over her. "What happened?"

Autumn held onto the bars of her cage. "I told you. He chained us. You can't get us out of here while we wear his chains. And you can't remove them by normal means. Only another dream weaver can remove them. Or the magic of one."

Elsie looked from Autumn to Jaxson with a glance at the other caged woman. They all had chains around their ankles. "There has to be a way." Her words were fierce and filled with the desperation she felt. "I can't-" She broke off with a guilty glance at Jaxson. She couldn't abandon him here yet again.

"Do you plan to become a dream weaver?" Autumn demanded.

"I don't even know what that means," Elsie said.

"Dream spinners would be drawn to you as they slept, bringing with them their unwanted possessions the moment you stayed in one place longer than six days. And you would be able to harvest the magic from their possessions, even if what they left was a person. Young or old, it wouldn't matter." Autumn's hand went to her stomach, fingers splayed as she rested it there. "Even the unborn."

Elsie took a step back from Autumn. "No. I don't want that."

"Then you can't help us," Autumn stated.

"Couldn't she stop being one after she rescued us?" Jaxson leaned against the bars, his head lowered. He slowly raised it, meeting Elsie's gaze. "Couldn't you become one for a short time so you can get us out of here?"

"Once done, it can't be undone," Autumn said. "Not that it makes all that much difference. Since she's a dream spinner, he'll be able to find her. He'll track her down through her dreams and bring her back so he can harvest her magic. She's his now. She shouldn't have woken and let him learn she knows of his existence."

Elsie drew in a sharp breath. There was no way she could go forever without sleeping. "There has to be another way."

"Find something he wants more than you." Autumn made a sweeping gesture that encompassed the room. "Something he wants more than all of us."

"How do I do that?" Elsie asked.

Autumn smiled, a humourless one that didn't reach her eyes. "I don't suggest asking him."

She started to demand what other way there was to find out, but decided the Dryad probably wasn't likely to be any more helpful than she'd already been. Which hadn't been much at all. "Thanks." She strode to the exit, her tone sounding the opposite of the word.

"Where are you going?" Jaxson reached through the bars towards her. "Don't leave us here."

She paused halfway up the stairs to look at him. He was still unrecognisable. Not even his mum would have known him if she'd stumbled across him. "I'll come back for you." She half turned away, going up a single step. "I promise." She turned her back on them.

"Your promises mean nothing," Autumn called out after her. "Without magic to bind them, they can be easily broken."

She headed for the corridor, hurrying along it as she glanced in each room, trying not to think of Autumn's words. Magic. She didn't want magic. Didn't want to have people randomly turn up in her house while they slept. How crazy was that? And she doubted her mum would appreciate strangers arriving in their sleep. Nor did she want to spend the rest of her life moving every six days. How far did you have to move? And could she return to a previous location, or would she be forced to never be in the same place more than six days at a time for the rest of her life? A shudder ran through her and she picked up her pace, almost running along the corridor.

At the sound of a crash ahead of her, she slowed her pace, straining to hear what was going on. Silence greeted her and she slowed further, barely moving. The end of the corridor was metres away, the door half closed and preventing her from seeing anything other than a patch of empty floor.

"You would try and break your promise to me?" the dream weaver bellowed.

If there was a reply, Elsie couldn't hear it. She stumbled forward the last few paces, peering around the edge of the door. Her mouth dropped open. The dream weaver held chains in his hands, his back to Elsie as he advanced on Caidon. The Fae appeared to be pinned to the floor by something invisible. She wanted to race in and set Caidon free, but there was nothing to free him from. Or at least nothing she could see.

"Well?" The dream weaver was quieter this time, stopping by Caidon's feet. "My magic is stronger than yours. There's no way you can escape. You're mine for the next decade and your sister's life is forfeit. Hers and her child's."

Elsie found herself throwing open the door and rushing into the room before she had the chance to think about her actions. "No." She shoved the dream weaver aside.

He'd half turned to face her, the chains clattering to the floor as he tried to keep his balance.

"No." She shoved him again, turning to grab hold of Caidon's hand as the dream weaver landed on the floor. "We have to get out of here."

"I can't travel anywhere. All I can see is this place." A dark green leaf formed in his hand, the peppery citrus scent filling the air around them. "Picture somewhere else. Hurry."

The dream weaver started to rise to his feet. "You're both mine."

"What do you mean?" Her grip tightened on Caidon's hand as the dream weaver gained his feet.

"Your room. See your room in your mind," Caidon ordered.

"I see it." Before she could ask why she needed to see it, the peppery citrus scent increased and the world shimmered, reforming as her room. She stared at Caidon, not sure what to ask him. There were so many questions.

Marinda threw herself at Elsie, dragging her away from Caidon as she wrapped her arms around her. "You're back. I had no idea what to tell your mum about you disappearing like that. I've spent hours trying to figure it out. Or even what to tell my mum. How could they get you back when I didn't know where you were? Don't you ever leave again. Do you hear me?"

Worried Caidon would leave and she'd never find her way back to Jaxson, Elsie tried to escape Marinda's tight embrace. "Don't go." She stretched a hand out to Caidon when she failed to escape from her friend. "Please don't go."

Marinda grabbed Elsie's arm. "What are you doing? Do you want him to take you away from here again?"

Elsie slipped out of Marinda's grasp, stepping away so she could put Caidon between them. "He didn't do anything I didn't want him to do."

Caidon stepped to the side. "I can't use my magic to travel anywhere without ending up back with the dream weaver. My promise means that every part of me wants to return there."

"Then why haven't you returned?" Elsie asked.

"I'll eventually lose the fight, but before then, I need you to help my sister escape," Caidon said.

"I tried." Elsie waved Marinda to silence when she started to speak. She glanced at her friend. "Later." She reached out a hand to Caidon, who sidestepped it. "They're chained."

Caidon momentarily closed his eyes, bowing his head before raising it and meeting Elsie's gaze. "Then there is no hope. Not for your friend and not for my sister."

"You found Jaxson?" Marinda demanded.

Again Elsie waved her friend to silence. "I don't believe that. Your sister said all we need to do is find something he wants more than all of us."

"There is nothing he wants," Caidon said.

"There has to be," Elsie stated.

Marinda glared at Elsie. "Will you stop shushing me? Now tell me what's going on. Jaxson is my friend too."

Elsie stared at Marinda, having no idea what to tell her. She barely knew what was going on.

"Well?" Marinda demanded.

"I don't know." Elsie's words were soft and her shoulders drooped as she spoke them. "I have no idea of anything."

"Then tell me exactly what happened and maybe I can help you figure it out," Marinda suggested.

Caidon looked Marinda up and down. "Are you a dream spinner too?"

Marinda shook her head.

"Then there's nothing you can do to help. Only a dream weaver, or a dream spinner who wishes to become a dream weaver, can help." Caidon turned to Elsie. "That's our best option. All we need is dream weaver magic. Pure magic, undiluted by other magic."

Chapter Ten

Elsie took a step back from Caidon. "No. I refuse to spend my life on the move, worried dream spinners will turn up in my location during their sleep."

"There are others who manage without having dream spinners disturb them all the time," Caidon said.

"But they have to move every six days."

"They have six locations they travel between, rotating between each one," Caidon said.

"How far apart do the locations need to be?" Elsie asked.

"Seventy-seven miles."

"What's that in kilometres?" Elsie asked.

Marinda took out her phone when Caidon shrugged. "It's a hundred and twenty-four kilometres. Well, it's just under that. Barely."

"Impossible. That'd take me over an hour to travel. How could I go to school? Not that my mum would let me wander around the countryside every six days on some sort of rotation," Elsie said.

"You wouldn't be able to live in this world," Caidon said.

"What?" Marinda demanded. "Why couldn't she live here?"

Elsie stared at Caidon, having been about to ask the same as Marinda. "You want me to give up my world?"

"You don't seem the sort who'd willingly kill someone," Caidon said.

Elsie recoiled from him like she'd been struck. "No."

"Are you crazy?" Marinda demanded.

Caidon advanced on Elsie, who retreated until the bed prevented her from backing away further. "Unless the dream weaver dies, we all belong to him. Me for the next decade and you, Autumn and Jaxson until you die. Is that what you want? To die. To let everyone else die."

She shook her head, words impossible to form. The word 'die' repeated in her mind that was awash with blood. Would that be how she went? Would there be litres of blood around her? That's how she always died in her nightmares. Endless amounts of blood. Nothing but blood.

Caidon held her hands, clasping them tightly. "Help me save my sister."

"I can't kill anyone." She met his vivid green eyes, wishing the plea she could see in them didn't make her want to agree to anything. "Caidon, I can't do it. Please don't ask it of me."

He released her hands, turning his back on her. "Then you're all doomed and I can never go home. How could I face my father after failing to save Autumn?"

She started to reach for him, wanting to comfort him. Wanting to apologise for causing him to fail. She lowered her hand before she could rest it on his back. She couldn't do what he wanted. Couldn't kill another, no matter the circumstances.

"Does it have to be Elsie who kills the dream weaver?" Marinda asked.

They both turned to face Marinda. Elsie gasped, shaking her head at the thought of her friend killing someone.

Caidon shook his head. "No, but I can't do it while bound by my promise and there's no way I can travel to my father's home and ask him for help. None of you know what his home looks like."

"Oh." Marinda's hopeful expression faded. "I was hoping you could." She made a face. "I'd like to offer, but I struggle to kill even a spider."

"There are those in certain locations of the realms of the Fae who would willingly kill for a price," Caidon said.

"I have no money." Elsie winced. "I mean, not that I'd pay an assassin or anything, but…" Her voice trailed off as she tried to think of how to explain herself.

"Again, none of you know any location that would allow me to seek help." Caidon turned to Elsie. "Is this world more important to you than your life?"

She opened her mouth several times, yet words still didn't come out. She tried again, shaking her head at her inability to answer him.

"What sort of life would she have if she became a dream weaver?" Marinda slipped an arm around Elsie's shoulders. "Some things can be worse than death."

"Becoming a dream weaver would not be worse than death." Caidon cradled one of Elsie's hands. "Please. I would owe you a life. My sister's life."

"What about the baby?" Elsie asked.

"Save them both and I'd owe you two lives." He continued to hold her hand between both of his. "Please, Elsie."

That hadn't been what she'd meant at all. "No, I–"

His hands tightened around hers. "I'd owe you the decade I would have been bound to him."

"No, that's–"

Again Caidon interrupted Elsie. "I can bind my promise with magic and swear never to harm you or have another harm you if you accept. The dream weaver never demanded that promise from me. Only complete obedience to what he asks of me."

She let out her breath in a rush of air. "Will you let me say what I'm trying to say?"

"I reckon you should just keep him talking," Marinda said. "The deal is getting better by the minute."

"I don't need you bound to me for a decade as my slave or whatever it is you'd be," Elsie said.

Marinda eyed Caidon. "Are you crazy? Look at him. You'd be the envy of everyone we know."

"But I wouldn't be able to live here," Elsie said.

"Oh, yeah. I forgot that." Marinda sighed. "That seems like a really bad bargain. There has to be another way to escape the dream weaver. And if one of you would tell me exactly what happened, maybe I could help figure this out."

Elsie drew her hand from Caidon's grip. "I'm not saying no, just that I want to see what the other options are first. Of course I don't want to die. I'm not crazy. I just don't know enough about your world to know what my options are."

"Oooh. Nicely worded." Marinda grinned. "Didn't some of that stuff we read say wording is important when dealing with Fae?"

"Once your friend knows what has happened, then will you decide what to do?" Caidon asked.

"No." Elsie wasn't about to make the situation worse by agreeing to something when she had so little information. "Then I will figure out what the next step is with Marinda's help."

"You better not let it take too long," Marinda said. "Your mum will be home any time. It's nearly midnight."

She stared at Marinda, her mouth open. Surely she hadn't been gone that long. "Impossible."

"Time is different between our realms," Caidon said.

Elsie momentarily closed her eyes, fighting back a groan. "This is getting worse by the minute."

"Is someone going to tell me what happened?" Marinda asked.

Elsie took a deep breath. If she didn't have much time until her mum came home, she better not waste it by having a nervous breakdown like she feared she was about to have. "I will." She rattled off everything that had happened, keeping her sentences short and abbreviating the details as much as possible. Caidon added a few comments, but other than that, she was the one to tell Marinda all that had happened.

"You have to take me with you," Marinda said. "This is better than aliens. Way better." She turned to Caidon. "What's your world like? Does everyone have magic?"

"Only the Fae and Demi Fae," Caidon said. "Not all humans in my realm have magic. Some have chosen not to and others have never been offered it."

"What else is different about your world?" Marinda asked. "And can I have magic? Will it hurt me?"

"There's too much iron in this world for you to remain here for any length of time if you have magic," Caidon said. "Any magic."

"Is that why I couldn't live in my world if I became a dream weaver?" Elsie asked.

Caidon inclined his head.

"Are you sure there's no way to get rid of the magic once I have it?" Elsie wanted to beg him to say yes.

"You can reduce your magic, but never completely rid yourself of it. That would allow you to remain here for longer periods of time, but not forever."

"I want it."

They both turned to Marinda at her words, only Elsie speaking. "Want what?"

"Magic," Marinda stated. "This is what I've been looking for all my life. The extraordinary." She indicated Caidon with a wave of her hand. "And here it is. The extraordinary. I knew it existed."

"You want magic." Elsie said the words slowly, not sure she'd heard correctly.

"Yes." Marinda gave a single nod.

"This isn't getting us anywhere," Caidon said. "I'll only be able to fight the magic binding my promise for so long before I'll be unable to resist returning to him. What do you want to do?"

"How long can you fight the promise?" Elsie asked.

Caidon shrugged. "If my magic was stronger, I might not have been able to fight against it at all."

"Can't you get rid of it, like you were saying when you were talking about living with iron?" Marinda asked.

"Then what would I do? Without my magic, or with only a very little of it, I'd be powerless," Caidon said.

Marinda shrugged. "Seems like you're powerless even with it."

Before Elsie could exclaim her friend's name, she heard the front door closing. "Mum's home." She dashed to her bedroom door, softly closing it and turning out the light. She kicked off her sneakers, leaving them beside the bedroom door. When a hand rested on her shoulder in the darkness, she nearly screamed.

"It's me." Caidon spoke near Elsie's ear. "What do you plan to do?"

"I don't know." She kept her voice as low as his.

"We're running out-" Caidon's words were interrupted by the door slowly opening.

Elsie stumbled back out of the way, putting up a hand to prevent the door from fully opening. She squinted at the light from her mum's phone. "You're home." She nearly groaned at the stupid comment.

"What are you doing awake? And in the dark?"

It took all her willpower not to glance over her shoulder to see if Caidon was out of view. "I need to use the toilet."

"Why aren't you in your nightwear?" Brenda asked.

"I guess I fell asleep talking to Marinda." She took a step forward, desperately wanting to pull the door closed behind her and glad she'd kicked off her sneakers. There was no way she could have explained why she was wearing them.

"In the dark?" Brenda's voice was filled with suspicion.

"Of course not in the dark. Marinda probably turned the light out." Elsie took another step forward.

Brenda stepped out of the way. "Are you okay?"

Chapter Eleven

Elsie nodded, wishing she could tell her mum everything that had happened. But there was no way she could convince her of anything. "I just need to use the toilet."

"You weren't woken by a nightmare?" Brenda took a few steps back so she could turn on the hallway light.

Elsie pulled the bedroom door closed behind her, worried her mum would see something with the amount of light now in the hallway. "Are you trying to wake Marinda?"

"I'm sure she wouldn't tease you about your nightmares," Brenda said. "You don't have to hide them from her. She'd be as protective of you as she is about your fear of blood."

"Mum! Do you want to give me nightmares?" She tried not to think of the images that word conjured and tried not to think about what Caidon would think of her mum's comments.

"Sorry. I'm worried about you. There's something wrong. I'm not an idiot. I just wish you'd talk to me about it." Brenda sighed heavily. "You used to talk to me about things."

She had no idea what to say. The truth would only have her mum worried even more. Not about the circumstances, but about her sanity. "They think I did something to him, don't they?"

"What?" The word burst from Brenda.

"The police. They think it's me. You heard them."

"Oh, Elsie." Brenda hurried forward and wrapped her arms around Elsie. "No one blames you."

She returned her mum's hug. "I didn't say they blamed me. It's more that they wish they could accuse me."

Keeping her arms around Elsie, Brenda drew back enough to meet her gaze. "No one would ever believe that of you. There's no way you could deliberately hurt someone."

"What about accidentally?"

Brenda didn't speak immediately. "Is there something you want to tell me?"

"No. I'm just saying what everyone is thinking."

"No one blames you or is accusing you of anything. Would you like to speak to a professional about how you feel?"

"No." She almost looked away from her mum's gaze, not wanting her to see any of the panic that suggestion caused. "I'm fine. I don't need to speak to anyone."

"Are you sure?"

She drew away from her mum. "Yeah." She looked in the direction of the bathroom. "I just need to use the toilet."

Brenda sighed heavily. "You know you can tell me anything."

"Yeah." She was sure her mum meant sane things. Believable things.

"I'll see you at breakfast."

"Okay." She didn't glance back when she hurried to the bathroom, staying in there longer than she needed. The hallway was empty when she came out and her bedroom door was closed.

There were no lights on in her room when she opened the door and she couldn't see anyone in there when it was filled with the light from the hallway. The only sign that either of them had been in there were the rumpled sheets on the mattress and bed and a peppery citrus scent. Had Caidon done something to Marinda?

"Are you coming in?"

Elsie jumped, pressing a hand to her heart as she turned to the right. She glared at her friend, who grinned at her. "Where were you?"

"I've been here all along." Marinda gestured to the spot at her feet, her grin not dimming. "Caidon hid us."

"How?" She stepped into the room, leaving the door open a fraction as she glanced around. "And where is he?"

Caidon stepped away from the wall. "I can't hide anyone for long and my ability only works on humans. Or at least those humans without magic."

Elsie made a startled sound as she jumped back, glaring at Marinda, who giggled. "Not funny in the slightest."

"Yeah, it is," Marinda said.

"Jaxson is still missing."

Marinda's grin faded at Elsie's words. "You're right. I'm sorry."

Elsie felt like she should be the one apologising at the guilty expression she'd caused to flit across Marinda's face. "We'll get him back."

"You'll become a dream weaver?" Caidon asked.

Elsie shook her head. "Your sister said something about using dream weaver magic to break their chains. Can it be used on them without needing to be used by a person? Or by a dream weaver."

"Can I become a dream weaver?" Marinda asked excitedly.

Elsie pressed a finger against her lips. "Don't forget my mum is home."

Marinda lowered her voice. "Sorry." She turned to Caidon. "Can I?"

"No. Only a dream spinner can become a dream weaver."

"What about your sister's boyfriend? Would he become a dream weaver and help us out?" Elsie asked.

"I don't know how to find him," Caidon said. "But from what I've heard about him, I doubt it."

Marinda turned on the light on her phone. "Close the door. I keep thinking your mum is going to catch us."

Elsie shut and locked her door. "How do we get dream weaver magic to use on the chains?"

"We'd need a drop for each chain," Caidon said.

"Three drops?" Elsie asked.

Caidon shook his head. "Six. One for each ankle."

"Can we get that much?" Elsie asked.

He shrugged. "It takes a lot to make a single drop and he usually puts it straight into a vial of Fae magic, increasing the power of it so he can sell it to the Fae or any others who might want more magic."

"I could buy magic from him?" Marinda asked. "How much does he charge?"

"He'd never sell it to one without magic. It'd be too big a risk," Caidon said.

"Why would it be a risk?" Elsie asked.

"They might be a human who's escaped from a powerful Fae and then he'd have that Fae after him," Caidon said.

"Can we get him in trouble with a powerful Fae?" Marinda asked.

"No. They'd have no reason to go against him." Caidon stepped close to Elsie. "If you truly want to save your friend, you'd become a dream weaver. For that you'd need but a single drop of dream weaver magic."

She wanted to say she would. Wanted to say she'd do anything to rescue the three captives. "I can't." She didn't want to leave her home. Her world. Didn't want to spend the rest of her life on some sort of rotation of locations. She wanted to live her life. Not keep hiding from the problems it seemed to constantly bring her. She shuddered as images of blood filled her mind.

"Elsie?" Caidon's voice was soft. "Is something wrong?"

"You've got that look on your face," Marinda said. "No one's hurt."

"What does that mean?" Caidon asked.

"You heard her mum in the hallway. Elsie is terrified of-"

Caidon clamped his hand over Marinda's mouth before she could finish the sentence. "Never tell another of your fears. Ever."

Marinda pushed him away from her. "Keep your hands off me."

"Then don't endanger your friend," Caidon said.

"Everyone knows she doesn't do any good at the sight of blood," Marinda said.

Elsie closed her eyes, wishing she could clamp her hands over her ears rather than hear that word. But surely she was too old to be doing something like that.

"Obviously not everyone. But if you are to come with us, you have to be more careful than that. Tell no one anything that can be used against you. We Fae will use any advantage, even an unfair one," Caidon explained.

"Why are you telling us this?" Marinda asked. "Now you won't have an unfair advantage over us."

"If I am to ally myself to you until my sister is safe, then I'm not about to risk another having an unfair advantage over one of you while we remain allies."

"I get to go too?" Marinda's expression brightened. "I get to go to your world?"

"I'll give you magic if Elsie will save my sister," Caidon offered.

Marinda turned to her. "Elsie! Did you hear him, Elsie?"

She wanted to protest. She met his gaze. "It looks like you aren't above using any advantage possible. Even unfair ones."

Caidon grinned fleetingly. "I'll do whatever possible to save my sister and her unborn child. And if you can save me a decade of misery, I'd do yet more to convince you to help me."

"We will get six drops of dream weaver magic." There was no way she was about to be the only one who lost out in this deal. "I never asked to be a dream spinner and I certainly don't want to become a dream weaver."

He held out his hand to her. "We don't always get to choose the hand fate offers us, but sometimes we can turn what we are offered into something better."

She placed her hand on his. "Meaning?"

"If you have Fae magic, then you can't become a dream weaver." He turned to Marinda and held out his hand, facing Elsie once Marinda had placed her hand in his. "Picture the dream weaver's home."

"I'm not ready to go there yet." Elsie tried to pull out of his grip.

Caidon tightened his hand around hers. "How else are you to gain dream weaver magic other than to go to a dream weaver and take it from them?"

"What about my magic?" Marinda asked.

Caidon's gaze remained on Elsie. "Once my sister is safe."

"Then leave Marinda behind. She doesn't need to go with us yet," Elsie said.

"No." Marinda grabbed for Caidon's hand when he let go.

Elsie tugged Caidon out of Marinda's reach, slipping her feet into her sneakers. "I'm picturing the house."

The peppery citrus scent filled the air and Caidon crushed the leaf he formed, causing the world to shimmer and reform. The two of them stood in front of the dark silhouette of the dream weaver's house. Above them, the sky was filled with stars and a single lamp sat in one of the tower windows, casting a long splash of light onto the grass below.

"How much time has passed?" Elsie stepped closer to Caidon.

Caidon shrugged. "Your friend isn't going to be happy when you return to her."

"Probably not, but she didn't need to be put in danger too." She let go of his hand when she realised she still held it, trying not to think of the dark forest that surrounded them. Were there beasts wandering amongst the trees? She pushed that thought aside, too. "How do we do this?"

"We need some vials." Caidon started towards the building.

Elsie hurried after him, grabbing hold of his arm and drawing him away from the door he was about to open. "Why a couple of vials?"

"One for my magic and one for the dream weaver's magic. This close to him I can barely contain the urge to go to him."

She saw the strain in his face in the limited light from the lantern. The way his jaw was clenched had her reaching for his face. She lowered her hand before her fingers made contact with his jaw. "Okay. Where will we find them?"

"There should be some in the kitchen." He cracked open the door, peering inside before fully opening it. "This way." He linked his fingers with hers, tugging her in after him before closing the door.

Chapter Twelve

This time Elsie didn't let go of Caidon's hand, not wanting him to go too far ahead of her. They paused at the other doorway, peering into the corridor before they turned towards the kitchen. There was barely enough light from the candles placed evenly along it, only some of them lit. Once in the kitchen, she reluctantly let him draw his hand away from hers and watched him rummage through cupboards in between glancing at the open trapdoor. The flickering flames in a fireplace were just bright enough for them to see by.

"Don't think about it." Caidon held out a vial to her.

She took it from him. "Think about what?"

"Going down to see your friend. We don't have time for that. You need to find a place to hide in the dream weaver's workroom. I'm sure by now he has one of his servants dealing with the dream spinners that arrive during the night so he can sleep." He took the cork out of the vial he held, cupping his hand beside it.

"Why do I need to hide in his workroom?" Her gaze remained fixed on his hand as it filled with a fine, white sand that had glittery specks of red, orange and green amongst it. "What are you doing?"

He tipped the sand into the vial, putting the cork into it. "Draining off some of my magic. I don't think a vial is going to be enough." He slipped the vial into a pocket of his trousers. "Let me find a couple more vials. He always brings them in here to clean them before he reuses them."

"You didn't say why I have to hide in his workroom."

He found three more vials, filling them as he spoke. "He works first thing in the morning. Even before he breaks his fast. He uses up some of the items from the night, taking the magic from them until he gains a single drop."

"You said we need six drops."

"We'll come back the next day."

"Won't he expect that?"

He pocketed the three filled vials. "Not the first two times. No one would expect us to return a second time. But after we've returned a second time, then he'd expect us to keep coming back." He took a step towards the corridor. "This way."

She glanced at the trapdoor before she followed him, wishing she could check on Jaxson before she hid in the workroom. Was he okay? Not that he'd really been all that well when she'd last seen him. But she needed to know he wasn't any worse. That he still lived. "Cai-"

He spun, clamping his hand over her mouth before she could say his name. He shook his head, pressing a finger against his lips before he drew his hand away from her mouth. When she opened her mouth, he again pressed a finger to his lips.

Sighing, she nodded, letting him know she'd be silent despite wanting to ask him why she couldn't speak. Even though she was certain a couple of the candles had gone out while they'd been in the kitchen, there was still enough light for her to see there was no one else in the corridor. Surely he could have let her say a few words.

He led the way back along the corridor, entering one of the rooms two doors along it. A set of spiral stairs led upwards and again he pressed his finger to his lips, waiting until she nodded before he lowered it and led the way up the stairs.

In the large room above, they stepped out of the doorway on the far side of it and directly into the tower, the curved walls further away from Elsie than she thought they should be. Another spiral staircase led upwards, a soft light falling on it from the room above.

Entering the room above, she stared around her at the many items crammed into the space. There were all sorts of things. Even the cushion from her couch. She started towards it, glaring at Caidon when he halted her movements. "That's mine." She pointed at the cushion, wondering if the sheet, cat ornament and book were also in here.

"It belongs to him now." He tugged her towards a workbench. "You need to see what he's doing here from where you hide. As soon as he gains a drop of magic, he'll add it to a jar of Fae magic."

She reached for the vial sitting in a contraption at the back of the workbench, a jar placed to the side. "What does this do?" The contraption had a shelf made of angled mesh, the angles meeting in a point that sat above the vial below.

"It guides the magic to the one point where it drops into the vial so he can pour it into the jar beside him." Caidon pointed out the parts as he spoke. "He'll tip a vial of Fae magic into the jar before he starts and after he's added his magic, the contents of the jar will rapidly increase until it's double the amount and stronger than it originally was. Everyone wants magic that has been altered by that of a dream weaver. He could live in a castle if he chose with the money he's earned. I have no idea why he stays here instead."

"Maybe he didn't want to become a dream weaver either." Her voice was soft, her gaze remaining on the contraption.

"You need to find somewhere to hide. I don't know how long it is until morning so make it somewhere you'll be comfortable."

She stared at the contraption a moment longer before she turned away, seeking a spot where she could hide and be reasonably comfortable while still seeing the workbench. When she found a spot, she grabbed the cushion and placed it behind a large dollhouse. "How would this have ended up here?"

"The same way as everything else. Brought to the dream weaver by a spinner."

"Who would take a dollhouse to bed with them?" She sat down behind it, peering through a back window at an angle that also allowed her to see through a side window.

Caidon laughed softly. "You dream spinners don't always fall asleep in your bed. A child brought this dollhouse, stretched out on their stomach with their hand resting against it."

She looked up at him. "Why wouldn't they want such a lovely dollhouse?"

Caidon shrugged. "Why wouldn't you want Jaxson?"

She met his gaze, opening her mouth only to close it straight away. What could she say? That Jaxson didn't make her heart race like he did? That maybe she was more like Marinda than she thought and had been looking for the extraordinary. She looked away, unable to keep meeting his vivid green eyes. "Where will you hide? There isn't enough room for two behind here."

He crouched in front of her, his fingers lightly touching her chin and turning her head to face him. "Why didn't you want Jaxson? Some of them who end up here you can understand instantly why they weren't wanted. But Jaxson has remained polite even when he was trying to escape me, apologising for hurting me during his attempt as soon as he realised I was as caught in this situation as he was."

"We should have remained friends, not tried to date each other."

"So it wasn't that you didn't want him in your life, you just didn't want him in that capacity in your life."

She nodded once, stopping when she nearly dislodged his finger from her chin. "We tried to be something to each other that we were never meant to be." She froze when she realised she'd leaned towards him, her gaze momentarily drawn to his lips. Would it be the same with Caidon? Would she find him to be only suited to being a friend within a month of dating him? Not that he was ever likely to want to date her.

He leaned in close, letting go of her chin to rest his hand on her shoulder. "I'll help you get him back."

His lips were so close that if she leaned forward only centimetres, hers would touch his.

"Elsie?"

She blinked several times, trying to focus on his words and not his lips. "Sorry. What did you say?"

"I asked if you would be fine here while I find a place to hide."

"Oh." She felt her cheeks heat. She'd been fantasising over kissing him while he'd been trying to comfort her. Clearly he wasn't at all interested in her as anything more than a temporary ally. She closed her eyes, barely managing not to groan.

"What is wrong?" He pressed a hand against her warm cheek, the other remaining on her shoulder.

Her eyes opened and she stared up at him. There was no way she was about to tell him what was wrong. "I'm okay. You find a hiding place."

"Are you certain?" He ran his hand across her cheek, brushing strands of her dark blond hair back from her face. "I can't promise I'll be able to protect you, not with how limited my magic is and the promise binding me to the dream weaver, but I can promise to try and help you if he tries to capture you."

She pressed her fingers against his lips. "No promises." She didn't deserve any from him. Not after all the problems she'd caused. "I won't have you bound further than you already are."

He turned his head slightly to dislodge her fingers before facing her again. "You care enough to want to keep me from being bound by further promises yet not enough to want to help me save my sister and her child."

"You misunderstood me earlier. I was trying to explain that I didn't expect any debt from you. That I wouldn't leave any of them caged. No one deserves that."

"You'll help me save my sister?" He twisted a lock of her hair around his fingers before releasing it and running his fingers along it.

The action reminded her of Jaxson. Except he never ran his fingers along the strands after he twisted them around his fingers. She closed her eyes, drawing in a deep breath.

"Elsie?"

She opened her eyes. "I'll help you save your sister and try to find what the dream weaver wants more than he wants a decade of you serving him."

"Why?"

The word was soft and she found herself leaning forward slightly, freezing when she realised there was barely a centimetre between them. "Because I do care."

"As a friend?"

She started to say yes, but couldn't bring herself to lie to him. Not when he couldn't lie to her. Although it wasn't a complete lie, it just wasn't the full truth. "Partly."

"And the other part?"

She found herself looking away, unable to keep meeting his gaze. "Aren't you going to hide?"

He turned her face towards him again.

She didn't raise her gaze.

"Elsie?" His lips slowly curved into a smile.

It almost made her meet his gaze. "What's so funny?"

His smile momentarily became a grin before it faded and his lips met hers, his hand that had been playing with her hair sliding around to the back of her neck.

Her hands slid around his waist as she returned his kiss, all the while telling herself she was crazy, that surely he meant nothing by the kiss and she was going to end up with a broken heart. But she couldn't bring herself to end the kiss. Found herself pressing closer to him instead, protesting when he drew away from her.

His hand that was tangled in her hair cupped the back of her head. "I need to hide, but when we're done here, I'd like to continue what we started."

Chapter Thirteen

Elsie stared up at Caidon when he let her go and rose to his feet, trying to think of something to say. All she could do was stare, dazed from the kiss and wanting to protest waiting to continue it.

"The moment you have the vial of magic, think of your bedroom and I'll take us back there."

"Okay." Her voice didn't sound like her own. It made her think of melted toffee. Warm and soft. Before she could clear her throat and try again, he was gone. She peered through the windows of the dollhouse. When she still couldn't see him, she leaned forward, looking around the edge. Had he used magic to hide? No. That didn't make sense. Magic wouldn't work on the dream weaver. She sat back down, trying not to think of the kiss. Thoughts of what she had to face filled her mind and she returned to thinking about the kiss. It seemed like the better option of the two. Although she might not think that once everything was over and she was suffering a broken heart. Caidon would return to his world and she'd be left behind in her own.

She closed her eyes, trying to ignore the wave of sorrow that washed over her. She should have been sensible and backed away from him instead of leaning in close. Drawing in a shaky breath, she tried to think of something else. Anything else. It didn't take her long to give up trying. The kiss had been amazing and even if he were with her for only a short time, she'd enjoy every second they had together. Walking away from him now, out of fear they'd end, was crazy. Nothing lasted forever. Or at least nothing rarely lasted forever. She should grab hold of him and make the most of the time they would have.

A smile slowly formed as she sank back against the dollhouse, reliving every second of the kiss. Her heart might eventually be broken, but she would certainly have some amazing memories to look back on at the end.

She had no idea how she went from thinking about the kiss to dreaming about a forest, the trees well spaced so that they let in dappled sunlight. Slowly turning, she tried to figure out where she was, other than in a dream. It was no forest she'd ever seen before.

"I knew you'd eventually have to sleep and then you'd be mine."

She spun to face the dream weaver, backing away from him as he advanced on her. "Leave me alone."

"You broke the rules. That makes you mine." He continued to walk towards her.

She kept backing away, her shoulder hitting a tree as she moved past it. "I wasn't told the rules."

"That's no excuse. Someone in your family was a dream spinner. They should have told you the rules."

She shook her head. She continued to back away from him, her retreat halted by a tree. "No one. Not one single person." She was the only one who ever lost things. She stepped around the tree.

"It runs in families. Not that you'd necessarily know who it was since dream spinners tend to have a short life."

Fear raced through her at his words. "You lie."

His lips twisted into a smile. "No one who has magic can lie. Not straight out. Avoid the truth, be ambiguous, repeat a lie that they believe is the truth, but never lie. One of your family members, or even several, is a dream spinner. Or possibly even a dream weaver if they're lucky."

"Lucky! What's so lucky about becoming a dream weaver?"

"You get to live instead of dying at the hands of a dream weaver. Although you probably wouldn't have noticed for a long time. As long as you remain unaware, you're safe. Someone placed a powerful enchantment on that ornament you brought to me. One that was broken by you bringing the human to me."

She ran into a tree again, remaining where she was instead of stepping around it. "Dad? It's Dad?" That didn't seem possible.

The dream weaver reached for her.

She dodged to the side, breaking into a run rather than stay to be caught. Her mind was full of questions. Her father was a dream spinner? That didn't make sense. How could he be a dream spinner?

"You can't run from me. This is a dream. I can create what I want to keep you from getting away."

She stumbled to a stop when a chasm appeared in front of her. Pebbles fell over the edge, not making a sound as they tumbled out of sight. She turned to face him. He strode towards her at the same pace as earlier. Not that he needed to go fast. There was nowhere for her to go.

"There's no escape from me. Ever. When I catch you in here, I'll be able to find you in reality."

She tried not to think of where she was, hidden in his building. If she didn't think of it, would that make it impossible for him to find her?

He stopped in front of her. "One touch and I'll know your location."

She couldn't let that happen. "Then I guess you'll miss out." She took a step back, screaming as the ground fell out from beneath her.

"Elsie. Wake up, Elsie." Caidon shook her, his hands tightly gripping her shoulders.

Gulping in air, she opened her eyes to stare up at him, feeling like she was still plummeting. "He was there."

"The dream weaver?"

She nodded.

"Did he get a hold of you?"

She shook her head.

"Are you sure?"

"I dropped into a chasm so he couldn't get me."

He crushed her to him. "That was crazy. What if you hadn't woken before you hit the bottom?"

"How do you know I didn't hit the bottom?" She rested her head against his shoulder, her arms slipping around his waist.

"Because you would have been harmed by the fall if you had."

She drew away from him, meeting his gaze, trying to figure out if he was joking. "Harmed?"

He nodded.

"By a dream?"

"By a dream that involved a dream weaver."

She drew in a shaky breath. "It would have killed me?"

"No, just injured you. Probably rather badly since you seem concerned you could have died."

His words didn't make her feel any better. "He said he could find me. That all he had to do was touch me and he'd know where I was."

Caidon inclined his head. "It's true. He can't lie. His magic prevents him from lying."

"He said that too."

"What else did he say?"

"That it runs in families." She took a deep breath, trying to sort through all her thoughts. "I think my father is a dream spinner."

"That bothers you?"

"Yes."

"Why?"

She held his gaze with her own, not sure if she should speak the words echoing in her head. When he ran his hand down her back, she closed her eyes. "I don't want to be anything like him." She opened her eyes when he remained silent.

"Having the same abilities as someone doesn't make you anything like them."

"I hope so." Again she closed her eyes, leaning forward to rest her head on his shoulder. "He's the last person I'd want to be like."

Caidon wrapped his arms around Elsie, holding her close. "You can be as much or as little like someone as you choose. It only takes time and a determination to change the way you act and think. You can form new habits."

"How about get rid of the ability to be a dream spinner?"

"No. That's a talent, not a habit."

"I need to talk to my father." She hated the thought of needing to have such a conversation with him. "Eventually."

"Maybe he can help you."

She snorted. "I doubt it."

"It might be worth asking."

"You don't know him or you wouldn't make that suggestion."

"I would like to meet-" Caidon broke off, drawing away from her. "Someone is coming." He pressed his lips against her forehead before he was gone, moving away at an unnaturally fast pace.

She wrapped her arms around herself, shivering at the loss of his warmth. It took her a moment to realise it wasn't so much the loss of his warmth since the room wasn't cold, it was more the loss of his comforting presence. She was alone in the dream weaver's workshop and didn't know if Caidon could reach her in time if the dream weaver found her. Not that she knew if he could help her against the dream weaver. All it'd take was the dream weaver to give him an order and he'd have to follow it.

Hearing someone enter the room, their footsteps light, she peered through the windows of the dollhouse. She wasn't able to see who'd entered until they reached the workbench. Her heart raced at the sight of the dream weaver placing objects on the angled mesh. He piled them up precariously, standing in front of the workbench with his hands raised and to the side, like he was ready to catch a large object.

He stayed perfectly still, his hands still raised and his back to Elsie. She wished now she'd found a different spot. One where she could see his face. Her gaze was drawn to the workbench and she breathed in sharply. He was between her and the vial, his body blocking the view no matter which window she peered through. She'd have no idea when there was a drop of magic in it. She looked from the dream weaver to the objects in the mesh several times. Would he hear her if she moved closer? Her gaze remained on the objects and she frowned. Had they faded?

She continued to watch them, her mouth dropping open as the colour slowly leeched away, a couple of the smaller objects becoming brittle and crumbling into dust that drifted to the workbench below. A glint of light appeared at the point of the angled mesh. She wished she could ask Caidon if it was the magic she waited for. But she had no idea where he was.

The glint of light slowly brightened, the objects continuing to fade and crumble. Peering through one of the upper windows, she could just see the top of the vial, where it sat below the point of the mesh. It was the same as the vial they'd taken from the kitchen. She wouldn't need that vial, only the cork from it. That was if she could manage to take the vial when the drop of magic fell into it.

The glint of light increased, gaining the appearance of a shining drop of water about to fall. Yet it held on, becoming larger and brighter. Elsie tried to remain relaxed, but it was impossible. She was tense and poised to dash forward and grab the vial. Could the dream weaver move as fast as Caidon? If he could, there was no way she could escape him. Her hands tightened into fists. She didn't want to be thrown in the cage again. Nor did she want to be stripped of whatever he took from people, draining them so they looked half dead, continuing until it killed them.

The drop hung lower, shimmering and quivering as it grew larger. Then it fell, seeming to do so in slow motion. Elsie dashed forward, snatching the vial from the dream weaver's grasp. She slipped the cork into place, throwing herself towards Caidon, who'd come out of hiding.

"Caidon!" The dream weaver glared at him, taking a step towards them.

Caidon formed a leaf as he grabbed Elsie's hand, the peppery citrus scent filling the air.

"I order you to bring me the-" The dream weaver's words were cut off as the world shimmered and reformed around them.

Chapter Fourteen

Elsie clung to Caidon's hand, trying to figure out what time it was by the amount of daylight in her bedroom, her heart still racing.

Marinda threw herself at Elsie, dragging her from Caidon's grasp. "I thought you'd never return. I had to tell your mum you were sleeping when she left this morning and send her texts from your phone on and off during the day. She wants you to ring, but I kept putting her off. Or you did, as far as she knows." She drew back to hold Elsie's phone out to her. "You better read the messages and give her a call. Before she comes home and checks on you like she threatened to do at one stage."

Elsie stared at the phone, heart still racing as she tried to make sense of everything.

"Elsie?" Marinda lowered her hand, still holding the phone. "Are you okay?"

"Yeah." Or at least she was as okay as it was possible to be in the circumstances.

"Are you sure?" Marinda studied Elsie. "You don't look that good. Was there bl-" She broke off with a glance at Caidon who prowled the room examining his surroundings.

"No. And I'm fine." When Marinda continued to look at her, Elsie sighed. "It runs in families."

"What runs in families?" Marinda asked.

"Being a dream spinner."

Marinda opened her mouth several times before she finally managed to speak. "There's someone else in your family who's one?"

Elsie nodded.

"Who?"

Elsie didn't answer immediately. "Possibly Dad."

"You've got to be kidding," Marinda exclaimed.

Elsie smiled, a wry one. "Yeah, my thoughts exactly."

"You going to call-" Before Marinda could finish her sentence, a message came through on Elsie's phone. She held it out to her.

Seeing it was from her mum, Elsie skimmed the messages that had been sent while she'd been in the realms of the Fae before telling her mum she could ring. She answered on the first ring. "You can stop worrying, Mum. I'm fine."

"Are you sure?" Brenda asked.

She thought of the vial of magic in her pocket. "Yeah. I am." Or at least she soon would be.

"If you're certain." Brenda sounded hesitant.

"Mum!" She put as much exasperation into her tone as she could. "Will you stop fussing?"

"I keep thinking about what you said early this morning," Brenda said.

"It's okay. I talked to Marinda about it. She agreed with you."

Marinda made questioning gestures.

Elsie shook her head, turning her back on Marinda. "So, I'm okay."

"I hope so."

Elsie smiled, trying to remain relaxed rather than think about everything she still had to do. "I am. So stop worrying."

"Call me if you need me."

"I will." Elsie said her goodbyes and disconnected the call once her mum had done the same. She took a deep breath, staring at the screen of her phone.

"What am I meant to have agreed with her about?" Marinda asked. "You know, in case she asks me about it."

"That the police don't blame me for Jaxson's disappearance." She couldn't take her gaze away from her phone. She really needed to ring her father. There were questions she had to ask him.

Marinda laughed. A short, sharp sound. "Oh, they totally do blame you."

Startled, Elsie looked up from her phone to meet Marinda's gaze. "You believe that too?"

"They asked about you in amongst all the other questions."

Caidon stopped his prowling to join them. "We should return as we don't know how much time will have passed between the realms."

Elsie checked the time on her phone. It was after two in the afternoon. Had they been in the realms of the Fae that long? She didn't think so. "How do you figure out the differences in time between your world and mine?"

"It's impossible. You never know how much time will have passed when you travel between the realms. Sometimes it can be barely any difference while at other times seconds can have passed in one realm while days will have passed in the other," Caidon said.

She drew her gaze from his to stare at the phone again. "I need to ring my father."

"You don't sound all that certain about it," Caidon said.

"It's not that I'm uncertain." She met Caidon's gaze again, momentarily focusing on his lips first. "It's just easier to have as little to do with him as possible. He always has these amazing ideas that he never thinks through." She tried not to think about the knife-juggling incident. Sadly, it hadn't been one of the worst of his ideas, only the worst one she'd witnessed.

Caidon rested a hand on her shoulder. "We can manage without his help if you think he'll cause more problems than he solves."

Marinda laughed. The same short, sharp one as earlier. "That's almost a given. Ron can screw anything up. Even the simplest of things."

"Elsie-"

She interrupted Caidon. "I have to call him. I need to know."

He nodded, lowering his hand.

She wanted to protest. Wanted to take hold of his hand and place it back on her shoulder. "I won't be long." She never was. They had little in common to talk about. Although that might be about to change. She dialled his number and waited for him to answer.

"Hey, sweetheart. You rang at just the right time."

She dreaded to know why, but he obviously expected her to ask. And he was likely to tell her even if she didn't ask, so she might as well get it out of the way. "I did? Why's that?"

"We're going white water rafting," Ron said enthusiastically.

"Oh?" That didn't seem so bad. It actually seemed quite ordinary considering it was her father she was talking to. Maybe he was finally getting his act together. Of a fashion.

"Yep, as soon as I pick up the surfboards. You wanna come?"

"Surfboards?"

"Yeah. It should be a blast," Ron said.

"You're going white water rafting using surfboards." Elsie spoke the words slowly, more for her own comprehension than his.

"Yep, that's what I said. You interested?"

She momentarily closed her eyes, letting her breath out slowly. So much for him getting his act together. "The word 'rafting' in white water rafting doesn't give you a clue on how it's done?"

Ron chuckled. "You definitely get your sense of humour from me. Your mum doesn't have a single humorous bone in her entire body."

She drew in a deep breath, deciding it was best to ignore his comment. Probably best to ignore the entire conversation that had occurred so far. "The words dream weaver and dream spinner mean anything to you?"

There was silence on the other end of the phone.

"Dad?"

"You still have that cat ornament I gave you?"

"Not anymore. It was taken from me. After I lost Jaxson."

"Lost him? In what way? Wasn't he kidnapped or something?" Ron asked.

"In a manner of speaking. Although I have been informed by the dream weaver that he was just taking what was owed to him." Elsie's grip tightened on the phone and once again her father remained silent. "Were you ever going to tell me?"

"I thought you liked cats," Ron said.

"I do, but that was the ugliest ornament ever made."

"You should have said."

She let out her breath in a rush of air, anger following on its heels. "Don't you dare make this my fault. You should have told me about them. You should have told me what the ornament was for."

"Yep, sure. And you'd have believed me as much as your mum did."

"You told mum?"

"Kind of. When I'd had one too many drinks. I'd lost my wallet. To the dream weaver. I tried to get my grandfather to help me out, but he said he'd done more than enough. As long as you're sleeping within a reasonable distance of the enchanted object, you appear unaware of the dream weaver. That's all you need to be. Unaware. There's another enchantment we can send with you that will make him forget you again."

"What about Jaxson?"

"It'll be too late for him. Besides, you obviously didn't want him anyway," Ron said.

She stood with her mouth open, the phone held to her ear. She drew it away and looked at it a moment before she placed it back at her ear. "You did not just say that."

"It's a pretty drastic way to get rid of a boyfriend, but it obviously works well," Ron said.

"I'm not leaving him there," Elsie stated.

"Take something from the dream weaver and the enchantment to make him forget you won't work," Ron warned.

"Then it's already too late." Her fingers brushed across the vial in her pocket.

"Why would you take something from a dream weaver? What were you thinking?"

"Maybe if you'd told me about all of this, I wouldn't be in this predicament," Elsie said.

"Was gonna get the enchantment put on that bracelet your great aunt gave you, but you lost it before I had the chance. Good thing though. Would have been a waste of effort getting it enchanted."

Chapter Fifteen

Elsie wanted to yell at her father, the anger still rolling through her. But it wouldn't help. "Your grandfather is a dream weaver?"

"Yep, your great grandfather. I asked him if he wanted to meet you, but he wasn't interested."

"I want to meet him." She didn't care if he wasn't interested. It wasn't like she'd asked to become a dream spinner. She nearly took the demand back when it occurred to her that for all she knew, the dream weaver after her might be her grandfather. Would it make a difference to him if he was?

"I'll let him know when I get back from white water rafting."

She was speechless for a moment. "You'll do what?"

"He's not that easy to get a hold of," Ron said. "I can only let him know and it'll be up to him if he wants to see you."

"You're going to wait until you're back from white water rafting?" Hearing the creak of the phone case, she loosened her grip.

"I've already arranged to go on this trip."

"You're going to leave me in danger of being taken by the dream weaver while you go off doing something stupid with your mates." She tried to unclench her jaw, but all she could do was talk through gritted teeth and try not to yell at him.

"You'd have fun. You should join us."

"You will let your grandfather know before you go white water rafting."

Caidon took hold of her other hand, gently squeezing it as he met her gaze.

Her anger didn't fade, but her control of it improved. "Do you hear me?"

"Hard not to. And it could take days. I've got to travel through one of the portals and leave a message for him. Then he'll send me a message of where to meet. If he wants to meet."

"Then do it. Your friends can wait. I can't." She doubted telling him how many of them couldn't wait would help, since he hadn't seemed at all worried about leaving Jaxson at the dream weaver's mercy. Which was a problem since he didn't seem to have any.

"You're so much like your mum at times," Ron muttered.

"So you'll do it? You'll get in touch with him?" Elsie persisted.

"I suppose I better, or I'll never hear the end of it," Ron complained.

"No. You won't."

"Was that all you wanted?" Ron asked.

She thought of and discarded several questions. She'd keep them for her great grandfather. If he bothered to meet with her. "Yeah, that was all."

"I was really looking forward to going white water rafting," Ron said. "It would have been a blast."

"You were looking forward to trying to get yourself killed?"

Ron chuckled. "Not any time too soon. Haven't you noticed we're hardier than most and heal quicker? About the only bonus to it all."

"What about your mates? Are they dream spinners?"

"Nah. You're the only other one I know."

"So you're letting them risk dying," Elsie said.

"That's their problem."

She could almost see the shrug he usually gave when using that tone of voice. "Call me when you hear from your grandfather." She hung up before she said something she regretted. Something that might make him change his mind about passing along the message.

"I could have told you it was a waste of time calling him," Marinda said.

"It wasn't. He agreed to pass along a message for me. That's all I need of him." She slipped her phone in her pocket.

"You need a lot more than that from him, but he's too useless to be a father to anyone," Marinda said.

Elsie drew in a deep breath and slowly let it out, trying to release the anger she felt. "I don't need him other than for this small task. I've never needed him. Mum and I do fine on our own."

"Does this mean we can return to my realm now?" Caidon continued to hold her hand.

"What if my great grandfather agrees to meet with me and we're not back so that I can?" Elsie asked.

Caidon formed a dark green leaf and held it out to Marinda. "Whisper a message to us against this leaf. But don't say my name or it will travel to me and you won't be able to contact us again."

Marinda stepped back from the leaf. "I'm going with you. You're not leaving me behind again."

Elsie took out her phone and held it up. "Take care of my calls and messages for me."

Marinda shook her head. "I'm not your secretary. You have to take me too."

Caidon let go of Elsie's hand and took out a vial of his magic. "I'll leave this with you. It's yours if you wait here and take care of messages for Elsie. Regardless of if Elsie rescues my sister."

Marinda eyed the vial. "What is it?"

"Magic."

Marinda took the vial before taking the leaf and phone. "How do I use it?"

"Tip it into your hand and wait for your body to absorb it." Caidon placed his hand on Marinda's when she started to open the cork. "Once you have magic, you can't lie."

"Oh." Marinda stared wistfully at the vial. "That's going to be a problem. At least while we're hiding all of this from Elsie's mum." She glanced at her friend before turning her attention to Caidon. "It doesn't go off or expire, does it? I don't have a time limit for when I can use it?"

"No. It will be fine to use decades from now."

Marinda grinned, slipping the vial into a pocket of her jeans. "Cool."

Caidon turned to Elsie, holding out a hand to her as he formed a leaf in the other. "Are you ready to picture the dream weaver's place?"

Her stomach rumbled. "Can't we eat first?" She also needed to use the bathroom, but that could be just because she was off on another journey. She always needed to use the bathroom just before a long car drive. Her mum complained it was psychological and unnecessary. Especially if she'd gone only half an hour before. She halted her meandering thoughts, trying not to think about what was ahead of them instead. "Well?"

Caidon lowered his hand. "It does make sense even though I fear for my sister's life."

"If we all help prepare something to eat, it shouldn't take long." Elsie strode towards the kitchen, hearing only Marinda follow. A glance over her shoulder showed Caidon followed too, but unlike Marinda, his footsteps were silent.

It didn't take them long to eat and use the bathroom and they returned to Elsie's bedroom before leaving. The world reformed around them and Elsie glanced around, the early light of dawn barely making it through the dense forest. "Are we too late?" Should they have gone without food?

"Think you can picture where you hid before?" Caidon crouched, tugging her down with him.

"Yeah." She could picture it right down to the windows in the dollhouse. How would the dream spinner have explained the loss of it? Or was that dream spinner lucky enough to have parents who had shared the information about their family's affliction?

"Ready?" Caidon asked.

She brought an image of the area to mind before she nodded. Again the peppery citrus scent filled the air and the world shimmered and reformed. She looked down at the cushion from her couch. She should have taken it back with her.

"He isn't in here yet," Caidon said. "Hopefully, the scent of my magic will fade before he is."

She made herself comfortable on the cushion, leaning against Caidon, who remained at her side, having shifted some things around first. "Why couldn't I smell that scent when the dream weaver was doing his magic?"

"Drawing magic from objects, and people, doesn't involve magic. Not for a dream weaver. It's a natural ability for them." Caidon wrapped a lock of her hair around his finger before releasing it and running the tips of his fingers along the length of a lock of hair.

She was tempted to do the same to his hair. "What is a dream spinner's natural ability?"

"To leave traces of dream magic in objects and people that they no longer want. They're like a net for the magic of lost dreams in their local environment. In a seventy-seven mile radius of them."

"Lost dreams?"

"Yes, the lost dreams of the humans around them. Some dream spinners put more magic into objects than others due to the people in their environment."

"What are the people like around me?"

"Hopeful. You live in a good neighbourhood. The objects you leave behind have very little magic in them."

"Is that a good thing?"

He briefly smiled. "Not according to the dream weaver. He prefers neighbourhoods filled with those who have given up on their dreams."

She started to ask another question, but he shushed her. Before she could ask him what was wrong, she heard footsteps. Her heart leapt, settling into a fast pace when she looked through the windows and spotted the dream weaver entering the room. She'd wanted to be in a better location this time, but it was too late for that.

The dream weaver glanced over his shoulder. "Place her on the draining shelf." He stood to the side of the workbench, arms crossed as he watched two men put the woman, who'd been caged, on the mesh. "Remove her chains." He tossed a key to one of them, taking it back once the man had finished with it.

The two men left, taking the chains with them while the dream weaver stood in front of his workbench, raising his hands.

It took Elsie a second to realise what he was about to do. Shaking her head, she rose to her feet. She wasn't about to let him kill the woman so she could have her drop of magic. She threw herself forward, avoiding Caidon who lunged for her, barrelling into the dream weaver. As he landed on the floor, she leapt onto the workbench, grabbing hold of the woman's hand. "Home. Take me home." She pictured her bedroom, holding her other hand out to Caidon as he leapt over the dream weaver who was rising to his feet.

The air filled with a peppery citrus scent as the dream weaver started to speak. Caidon crushed the leaf he'd formed and the world shimmered and reformed as Elsie's room. He let go of her hand to grab the woman who dropped towards the floor, catching hold of her before she landed on it. He lowered her to the carpet, looking up at Elsie from where he crouched. "We won't get the chance to take another drop from him."

"I know." She had no idea what they could do now. "It would have killed her, wouldn't it?"

Caidon nodded.

Marinda stepped into the bedroom, freezing when she saw the three of them. "Who is that? Is this your sister?"

Caidon shook his head, helping the woman sit up when she struggled to do so.

"Then who is she?" Marinda demanded.

"I didn't believe you'd come back for us," the woman said. "Jaxson kept saying we could trust you, but Autumn and I didn't believe him."

"Do you have somewhere you can go?" Caidon asked. "A home you can return to?"

"Won't the dream weaver find me?" the woman asked.

"I can give you a pinch of my magic. Just enough to change what you would be to him, but not enough to bother you around iron for years to come. It'll be up to you to find your way to a portal and back to the realms of the Fae before then."

"What if I don't want to return to your world?" the woman asked.

"The only other option is death at the hands of the dream weaver," Caidon said. "Or dying from iron sickness."

"Jaxson will need to have magic, too?" Elsie asked.

Caidon nodded.

"What about your sister?"

"She'll be safe when she sleeps, as long as she does so in her tree. He won't be able to reach her there. Her or her unborn child," Caidon said.

Chapter Sixteen

"They'll all be safe once we get them away from the dream weaver?" Elsie asked.

Caidon nodded before returning his attention to the woman. "If you can picture your place in this realm, I'll be able to take you there. After a quick visit to my realm first."

"Why do we have to go back first?" the woman finally made it to her feet, leaning heavily on Elsie's arm rather than take the one Caidon offered.

"I can't use magic to travel directly to a destination in this realm. It must be done from my realm," Caidon explained.

"Will I be able to travel like that once I have magic?" Marinda asked.

Caidon inclined his head. "Possibly. With practice."

"Will you teach me?" Marinda begged. "Please."

"We'll talk about it later," Caidon said.

"That's usually a no." Marinda's shoulders slumped. "Every time my mum says that, it's always a no."

"In my realm, that's the offer to negotiate with some-one," Caidon said.

"But I don't have anything to negotiate with," Marinda protested.

Caidon smiled. "You never know. Sometimes you humans have no idea of the value of the things you possess."

Marinda's expression brightened. "Really?"

"I'm not promising anything." He turned to Elsie, holding out his hand. "You'll need to picture my realm so I can take us there before we return to this realm."

She'd no sooner told him she was picturing the dream weaver's building than he was taking them there, quickly taking them away as soon as the woman could picture her home. They appeared in a darkened room, leaving the woman behind when they returned to the realms of the Fae.

Caidon formed another leaf when Elsie said she was ready, remaining where he was.

"Is something wrong?" Elsie asked.

Caidon didn't answer her immediately. "Your friend gives too much information when she uses the leaf to whisper to me. Your mother is home and Marinda told her you've gone for a walk and left your phone behind because you wanted a break from all the messages. You need to travel to somewhere outside your house. Somewhere no one will see us appear."

She thought of and discarded several places, finally settling on a dark alley running between two high-rise buildings, several blocks away, in the next suburb. She'd chased a note she'd dropped into it one day and had been keen to get out of it as quickly as possible. It had given her the creeps the way so little light reached the ground due to the angle of the buildings. "I'm ready."

The world shimmered and reformed, the alley darker than Elsie remembered. She tugged Caidon towards the exit.

"How far is your home from here?" Caidon matched her pace.

"Maybe ten minutes."

"Where do you want me to wait for you?"

"What do you mean?"

He brushed his hair back from his ears. "I can't exactly turn up looking like this."

Her frown cleared and she grinned up at him. "You're in a play. A Midsummer Night's Dream. It takes too much effort to put the ears back on so you've left them on until the end of the play."

"I can't tell her that. Remember, I can't lie," Caidon warned.

She swore. "That's going to make it harder."

He lightly squeezed her hand. "I take it you don't want your mother to know any of what has been going on?"

"She'd think I was going insane."

"I can prove it to her," Caidon offered.

She thought on it, eventually shaking her head. "No. At least not yet. If I'm lucky, I'll be able to sort all this mess out and she won't have to know a thing. She worries too much as it is."

"Then I'll do what I can to make sure she doesn't learn of it from me," Caidon said.

This time it was her that lightly squeezed his hand. "Thank you."

"I'm the one who owes you," Caidon reminded her.

"You don't. I'd say we're in this together. Equally."

He drew her to a stop, tugging her towards a two metre high fence that ran along the footpath and blocked most of the view of the two-storey house set behind it. "Together?"

"I'm not sure what you're asking."

"What happens when the dream weaver is no longer after you? Will you still want me in your life?"

"Will you still want me in yours?"

He smiled briefly. "I was the one who asked first."

She glanced away, not sure what to say.

"You can tell me how you feel. I'd rather have the truth than a lie," Caidon said.

"I don't want to lie to you when you can't lie to me." She met his gaze again, staring into his vivid green eyes.

"There can be ways around the truth."

"Have you lied to me?"

"Only when I insinuated it was a dream."

"How could you speak that lie?"

"Because it was a single word. Nothing more, nothing less. There was no information. Just a word you dream spinners take to mean you're dreaming. It could just as easily be me telling you it was time for dreaming."

"That seems really complicated."

"We Fae love complications. Now tell me, do you want me in your life once the dream weaver no longer hunts you?"

She ran her fingers down his cheek, smiling when he captured her hand and pressed her palm against his lips. "How old are you?"

"Twenty. How old are you?"

"Seventeen. I was worried you might be old."

He chuckled. "We do begin our lives as babies, like humans do. We just live a good bit longer than you tend to."

"How much longer?"

"Hundreds of years." He pressed her palm against his lips again. "I'm hoping I can convince you to have magic so your future will be as lengthy as mine will potentially be." He sighed. "Your friend sounds panicked. Your mother wants to call the police."

She drew her hand away from his. "We better hurry up then." When he started to take a step away, she drew him back, meeting his gaze. "And I do want you in my life once the dream weaver no longer hunts me."

He grinned, crushing her to him and kissing her thoroughly before drawing back to stare down at her, his arms around her waist. "Your friend won't be silent."

It took a few seconds for his words to make sense. "We better go." The last thing she needed was the police questioning her again.

They strode along the footpath at a fast pace, reaching Elsie's home just over ten minutes later. Brenda pulled open the door as they approached, her arms crossed over her chest.

Elsie's steps slowed and she was glad she'd let go of Caidon's hand when they'd entered her street. She spoke as soon as she was close enough for her mum to hear her. "I needed a break."

"Marinda didn't tell me you went for a walk with someone."

"Caidon's a friend. I ran into him while I was out." She tugged the hair back from his ears. "Aren't they cool? He's in a play. 'A Midsummer Night's Dream.' He gets to keep them until the play's over."

"Do you know each other from school?" Brenda asked Caidon.

He spoke before Elsie could say anything. "Through a mutual acquaintance."

"He knows Jaxson," Elsie said.

"Oh." Brenda stepped back to let them enter. "I'm sorry your friend is missing."

Caidon inclined his head. "Thank you."

"Are you staying for dinner?" Brenda asked. "There's enough to feed one extra."

"It's nearly dinner time?" Elsie exclaimed.

"How long were you out?" Brenda asked. "And what happened to not going anywhere alone?"

She had no idea what to say. Or more accurately, what Marinda had said.

"It's probably my fault she was out so long," Caidon said.

"We were talking," Elsie said. "About Jaxson." She had no answer for the other question since she technically hadn't been out alone.

Brenda led the way to the kitchen, glancing over her shoulder. "You will take your phone with you in future. I don't care how much you think you need a break. It's not safe to wander around without some way of contacting help if you need it. In fact, I want you to stick to the original plan of not going anywhere alone."

"Sorry, Mum."

Marinda met them in the doorway of the kitchen, holding out Elsie's ringing phone. "It's Ron."

"What does he want now?" Brenda demanded.

Elsie took the phone before her mum could, worried about what she might say to him. "Yeah?"

"He'll see you."

"When?"

"He sent a pebble for you to use. You step on it to crush it and it takes you to him," Ron said.

"Alone?"

"Three can travel with it. You're not expecting me to go with you, are you?"

She should know better than to expect anything from him. "No."

"Good. I've still got time to make it to the river before they leave without me. I'll drop it off on the way."

"I'll see you then." She disconnected the call, wishing her mum hadn't been standing beside her, listening to her side of the conversation. There'd been things she'd wanted to say.

"What does he want?" Brenda asked.

"He's taking me to meet my great grandfather."

"What? The old man died when your father was a boy. What's he trying to pull?" Brenda demanded.

"I guess the conversation makes more sense now. He's feeling nostalgic or something. Wanted someone to visit with him. I think he was talking about a cemetery at one stage," Elsie said.

"He better not have been drinking. You're not going anywhere with him if he's been drinking," Brenda warned. "And what about dinner?"

"We should have enough time to eat before he gets here." Elsie slid her phone into her pocket. "And I'd never get into a car if the driver has been drinking. I know better than that."

"Maybe I should go with you." Brenda strode to the stove, glancing over her shoulder as she spoke.

"I'm fine. Caidon and Marinda can go with me." She wished she could leave Marinda out of it, but there was no way she could explain taking Caidon and not Marinda.

"That doesn't make me feel all that much better." Brenda checked inside the oven, closing the door before taking plates out of the cupboard.

Marinda grabbed hold of Elsie's hand, grinning at her and squeezing her hand.

Chapter Seventeen

Elsie wished she could warn her friend to restrain herself. She didn't want her mum questioning what was going on. And she needed to warn her father about the cover story in case her mum went out to the car to talk to him.

It wasn't until they were seated at the table, and Brenda had to take a call from her boss, that Elsie had the chance to text her father and let him know what she'd told her mum. He sent a text back, wanting to know how he was meant to go white water rafting when the three of them were coming with him. He didn't have that many surfboards.

Marinda peered at Elsie's phone. "That doesn't make sense. What do surfboards have to do with white water rafting?"

Elsie replied to the text, letting him know he could drop them a couple of streets away at the local park. "You really don't want to know."

"Of course I do," Marinda said.

Hearing her mum returning, Elsie briefly pressed a finger to her lips.

Marinda sighed. "You do know I will ask again later."

Elsie grinned. "Yeah. I know." But that didn't mean Marinda would get an answer.

Ron arrived while they were cleaning up after dinner, hitting the horn rather than coming to the door. Brenda glared in the direction of the front door. "Typical. He always arrives at the worst possible time."

Elsie hugged her mum. "I'm not sure how long we'll be, but I suppose Marinda and I will head to bed the moment we get in. It'll probably be late, knowing Dad."

Brenda's arms tightened around her. "Take care. And don't go with him if he's been drinking."

"I'll take care and don't worry. I have no plans to get into a car with a drunk driver. Not even Dad." She let go of her mum, giving her a reassuring smile before she grabbed Marinda and Caidon's hands and headed for the front door. She was pretty sure, from her mum's expression, that her smile hadn't reassured her in the least. Not that she was surprised, considering her father's track record.

Ron hit the horn again as they reached the front door, stopping when the door swung open. The moment they were all in the car, Elsie in the front and the other two on the back seat, Ron pulled out onto the street. His gangly figure looked like it was too tall and angular to fit comfortably in the medium-sized sedan. "Someone direct me to where the park is? I need to get going or I'm going to miss out on catching up with everyone." He held a shiny black pebble out to Elsie.

She took the object, pointing up the road. "First turn to the left." She glanced at the pebble. "What do I do with this?"

"Crush it beneath your foot while holding onto the hand of everyone you want to travel with you." Ron glanced in the rear view mirror. "You hanging out with Fae these days? You do know they can't be trusted, don't you?"

She glanced at her father. "There are a lot of people I wouldn't trust, but Caidon isn't one of them." She remained silent other than to give directions to the park, not interested in being part of the conversation between Marinda and Ron about white water rafting with surfboards. She got out of the sedan the moment Ron pulled over.

He grabbed hold of her wrist, preventing her from moving away from the vehicle. "He'll probably want something in return for helping. He always does. Don't offer, see what he wants instead. No need to give him any more than you have to. That's providing he is interested in helping. He might say no to whatever you ask of him."

"Thanks." She pulled out of his grip, closing the door as she stepped away from the car.

"What did he want?" Marinda nodded towards the car as it pulled away.

"Supposedly to be helpful." At least she assumed that was what her father had been trying to be. It wasn't something he did very often.

"He should have done that while you were still sitting down rather than risk you falling over from shock."

Elsie grinned at Marinda's comment. "Pretty much." Her grin faded as she looked at the pebble she held. "Are we all going to visit him?"

Marinda linked her arm with Elsie's. "You're not leaving me behind again."

"It'll probably be dangerous." Elsie warned.

"So?" Marinda demanded.

Elsie smiled at her friend. "Okay. I won't leave you behind."

They headed for a cluster of trees, deep shadows beneath them, light from the scattered lampposts not reaching far beneath their widespread branches. Once beneath them, Elsie dropped the pebble on the ground before taking hold of Marinda and Caidon's hands.

Marinda tightened her grip on Elsie. "I'm ready whenever you are."

Elsie turned to Caidon. His nod was just visible in the shadows. "Okay. Let's get this over and done with." She crushed the pebble beneath her sneaker.

The world shimmered and reformed around them. They were in what looked like a rubbish dump. Around them items towered in uneven piles, creating a random maze for them to wander through. "How are we meant to find anyone in here?" Marinda demanded.

"You could call out for me."

They all spun to face the unfamiliar voice. Elsie stared at the young man who reminded her of her father. "You're my great grandfather?"

"Yes, yes. I know I look ridiculously young. Deal with it and move on, why don't you?"

"I think ridiculously young is an understatement," Marinda said. "You look about as young as us."

"You requested an audience with me, not the other way around."

"I don't even know what to call you," Elsie said. "Great grandfather? Just grandfather? Or would you prefer something else?"

"Harold will do. Now why did you want to see me?"

Elsie felt weird thinking of him by his first name. But it also seemed odd to call him grandfather when he looked so young. "Is there a way to stop being a dream spinner?"

"Only by becoming a dream weaver. I'll make you the same offer I've made all my descendants. A single drop of magic to do with as you will. Become a dream weaver or not, that's up to you." He held out a vial, the familiar gleam of dream weaver magic filling the bottom.

Elsie took the vial from him. "I actually need-" She broke off, having been about to say six drops, but they'd rescued one of the captives. "I need four drops of magic." Before she could correct herself again, and say that with the one he'd given her, she still needed another two, Harold spoke.

"You'll accept the single one I'm willing to offer and be grateful I've given you that much. Most dream weavers wouldn't bother."

"Then why are you?" Marinda asked. "What's the catch?"

Harold glanced at Marinda before focusing on Elsie again. "Does she speak for you?"

"Not really, but I would like to know the answer to her question," Elsie said.

"A promise I made to someone a long time ago. And it doesn't cost me anything to uphold it." He took a step back. "Is that all you wanted? I have things to do. The piles of lost dreams never grow any smaller and I'm well behind in harvesting magic from them."

"What if I trade you something in exchange for another two drops of magic?" Elsie asked.

"I'm currently not in need of anything," Harold said.

"What about something you might want rather than need?" Elsie suggested.

Harold made a sweeping gesture that encompassed the towering piles around him. "Does it look like I'm lacking anything or lacking the means to gain what I want?"

Elsie wanted to beg him to help further, but it was clear to see he wasn't interested in talking to her, let alone helping her. "How do we return home?"

He held out a pebble, the same as the one she'd crushed. "It'll take you back to where you left from."

"Thank you." Elsie took hold of Caidon's hand first. "What if I should need to get in touch with you again?"

"You're as bad as your father." He tossed another pebble to her. "Don't pester me too much or you'll regret it."

Elsie caught the pebble and slid it into her pocket, biting back the sarcastic comment she wanted to make. "Thanks." She managed to keep the sarcasm from her tone, but not the dryness.

Marinda linked her arm through Elsie's. "He's not much of a grandfather."

"I never planned to be one. Being a father wasn't exactly suited to me either." Turning his back on them, he strode away, disappearing amongst the towering piles.

Elsie dropped the pebble by her sneaker. "Are we ready to go?" They needed to figure out how to get more magic and standing around here wouldn't help with that.

"Might as well," Marinda muttered. "This was really disappointing. I thought it'd be more interesting."

"You want interesting, try being hunted by a dream weaver." Elsie stepped on the pebble, crushing it. The world shimmered and reformed as the park where Ron had dropped them.

Marinda let go of Elsie's arm. "This is kind of cool. Being able to travel around with magic. But everything else seems ordinary. And no, I don't want to be hunted by anyone to make things more interesting. That'd be the wrong kind of interesting."

"Who are we going to use the dream weaver magic on?" Caidon asked. "Or are you going to use one of them on yourself so you can set both of them free?"

"There have to be other dream weavers. If we find one, we can take magic from them before they can add it to Fae magic," Elsie said.

"How many dream weavers do you want hunting you down?" Caidon asked.

"I can have your magic afterwards and it won't be a problem." Elsie tucked the pebble into a pocket, hoping she never had to use it. "Just enough magic that I can stay in my world for another couple of years while I try to figure out what to do next. Surely I can come up with something better than being hounded by dream spinners for the rest of my life."

Marinda took out her phone, gasping. "It's nearly dawn. How can that much time have passed? We were barely gone for long at all."

"We need to get home so we can head back to the realms of the Fae." Elsie strode towards the footpath, Caidon remaining at her side.

Marinda hurried after her, walking at her other side once she caught up. "I want to go with you."

"No." Elsie wasn't about to risk her friend any more than necessary. It was bad enough that Jaxson was caged. She didn't need Marinda caught too.

"Oh, come on," Marinda protested.

"I can't take two with me or I won't be able to take anyone else with me when we set one of them free." Caidon glanced at Elsie. "Who are we setting free?"

"Jaxson."

"What about my sister?"

"Maybe we can take some of her tree to her, like you said," Elsie suggested.

"Do you plan to help her at all?"

Chapter Eighteen

Reaching the footpath, Elsie stopped, turning to face Caidon. "Of course I'll help your sister. I'm not about to leave anyone behind. It's wrong that people can be left behind for the dream weaver. There has to be a way to prevent it."

"It's up to each individual dream weaver what they do with the people brought to them. Some turn them into pets, others servants and a handful more drain them of all magic and also life. Very few of them set them free." Caidon gestured in the direction of Elsie's home. "Are you ready to return now?"

Elsie didn't feel at all ready. "Yeah. Let's go get Jaxson so his mum can stop worrying about him."

"And maybe my mum will stop panicking." Marinda walked on the other side of Elsie, not holding her hand like Caidon was.

Elsie was conscious of Caidon at her side, his hand in hers. She felt bad about not helping his sister first, but surely she had the better chance of surviving since it was her world. Not knowing what to say and not wanting to risk him trying to convince her to save his sister first, Elsie remained silent until they reached her house. "No one talk so we don't wake my mum."

They quietly entered the house. Elsie was relieved her mum appeared to have gone to bed. There was no way she was ready to face that interrogation. But maybe if they had something else to talk about, like Jaxson's return, her mum might not be so worried about where she was all the time. Reaching her bedroom, she held the door open until they were all inside, about to close it when she heard a sound.

Glancing along the hallway, she saw her mum walking towards her. She nearly groaned. "Marinda and I tried not to wake you."

"I wasn't asleep. Did you think I'd sleep properly until you got home?"

She shrugged instead of answering, since that was exactly what she'd thought. "I'll see you when you're back from work. I plan to sleep half the day away." She forced a yawn, that quickly became real. "I'm tired."

Brenda studied her. "Is everything okay?"

"Yeah. Just tired. Like I said."

"And your father?"

"Same as always."

"Did you-"

Elsie interrupted her mum, not wanting to drag the conversation out any further. "I'm tired."

Brenda didn't answer immediately. "I'll see you in the morning." She hesitated a moment before she turned away.

Elsie slipped inside her room, leaning against the door and listening to the sound of her mum's footsteps.

"What do you want me to tell your mum when she wakes up?" Marinda asked once everything was silent again.

"Pretend you know nothing," Elsie said. "It'll probably be easier that way."

"But that means you'll get in trouble," Marinda protested.

Elsie shrugged. "There are worse things." She tried not to think about the dream weaver, but thoughts of him invaded her mind anyway. "Far worse things."

"I can probably string her along like I did yesterday," Marinda offered.

"It's okay." Elsie handed her phone to Marinda. "Look after it for me." She didn't want to risk anything happening to it in the realms of the Fae, especially since they might have to face the dream weaver again.

"Be careful." Marinda hugged Elsie tightly before stepping back. "And bring Jaxson home."

"I'll try." She had no idea which comment she was answering, but she supposed the reply worked for both of them. She moved closer to Caidon, taking his hand. "I'm picturing the front of the dream weaver's place."

Caidon crushed a leaf before Elsie had finished speaking and the world shimmered and reformed. It was the middle of the day, the sun directly overhead and sunlight managing to reach some way into the forest where it pressed up around the building.

She wanted to run. Wanted to return home and forget she'd ever had the idea of trying to rescue Jaxson. It was madness. Someone was going to get hurt and it would likely be her. She remained where she was. Neither advancing nor retreating.

"Did you want me to set him free while you wait out here?" Caidon asked.

She shook her head.

"Don't you trust me to set him free rather than my sister?"

"I do, but I shouldn't expect you to go into danger while I stay out here kind of safe." She stared at the front door, still unable to bring herself to take a step towards it.

"Are you not going to save your friend?"

"What if he's not in the cage? What if we're too late and the dream weaver has taken all the magic from him and killed him in the process?"

"There's only one way to find out." He gestured towards the door.

She briefly closed her eyes, trying to convince herself to take a step forward. But it was hard. All she wanted to do was beg Caidon to take them away from here. Taking a deep breath, she straightened her shoulders. He was right. There was only one way to find out if she was too late.

The room was empty, as was the corridor when they peered into it. The place was quiet and they made their way silently to the kitchen. It too was empty. Elsie's stomach turned and she felt like she might be sick. What if the cages were as empty as everything else? She stared at the trapdoor, unable to bring herself to take another step.

Caidon tugged her towards the trapdoor, his grip on her hand firm.

She wanted to pull away from him, but she'd told Jaxson she'd return. Reaching the top of the stairs, she peered down them, a wave of relief having her swaying on the spot. Both Jaxson and Autumn were in the cages, no one else with them. Letting go of Caidon's hand, she hurried forward, grabbing hold of the bars to stare in at Jaxson, who remained lying on the floor.

He didn't move. "I knew you'd come back for us."

She dreaded having to tell him she could only rescue one of them.

"Take Autumn out of here first, then come back for me," Jaxson said.

Caidon remained at the bottom of the stairs. "We only have enough dream weaver magic to free one of you."

Autumn came to her feet, grabbing hold of the bars. "Who gets left behind?"

Jaxson struggled to rise, giving up after a couple of attempts, remaining lying on the floor. "Leave me behind. Take Autumn first." He paused a moment. "Her and the baby."

Elsie wanted to argue his statement, but she knew him well enough to recognise his expression. "I don't know how long it'll take to get more dream weaver magic."

"He said there's another two or three drops of magic left in me. You have time."

The words caused her to draw in her breath sharply. "Jaxson-"

"It has to be me who stays. I couldn't stand it if something were to happen to Autumn. Besides, there's two of them and only one of me."

"Happen to her? You…." Her voice trailed off rather than say the words 'love her'. "You've known each other for so little time."

"Two weeks. Or an eternity," Jaxson said.

"You've been here that long?" The words burst from her. "I'm sorry. I didn't know."

Jaxson closed his eyes, his voice soft. "If you don't make it back in time-"

Elsie didn't want to hear the rest of his comment. "I will." Letting him speak his final words felt like letting him give up.

"But in case you don't, can you tell-"

"Jaxson, don't you dare give up." Her grip on the bars tightened and she wished she could take both of them.

He opened his eyes. "I'm not giving up. Just being realistic. He'll eventually come for me. It's easier taking magic from people than from objects. He told me that."

She wanted to tell him he was wrong. She'd be back for him before the dream weaver came for him. But she couldn't bring herself to lie. There was a chance she wouldn't get the magic in time.

"We can't stay down here too long. If a dream spinner brings someone with them, we'll be caught when they bring that person down here," Caidon warned.

"Tell my mum I'm sorry," Jaxson said. "She'll be all alone if I don't make it back. She hates being alone. Tell her I'm sorry."

She tried to say something. Anything. But words wouldn't come. Instead, she nodded, meeting his gaze for a moment before she turned to face Autumn. The Dryad looked a little pale, but other than that seemed fine. "He hasn't taken magic from you?"

"Not since Caidon struck a deal with him," Autumn said. "But it's only a matter of time before he starts again." She rested her hand on her stomach. "We wouldn't last long. Not with how much he'd already taken before he stopped and how little magic the dream spinner left behind in me."

Letting go of the bars, Elsie moved closer to Autumn. "I need to put a drop of magic on each of the chains at your ankles."

Autumn pressed herself against the bars, turning sideways so Elsie could easily tip the contents of one of the vials onto the chain at her ankle. When it fell away, she turned so Elsie could deal with the other one. "Thank you."

"We're not out of here yet," Elsie warned.

Autumn held out a hand to her brother. "You can take us out of here. We don't have to wait for a dream spinner this time."

Elsie eyed the faint glimmer left in the vials. "There's a little bit of magic left. Would it be enough to break Jaxson's chains?" She tried to use a finger to get it out, but the vial was too narrow.

Caidon grabbed her hand, drawing her to her feet. "If you touch the magic, even so little a bit as that, you risk becoming a dream weaver."

She nearly dropped the vial at his words, fumbling to keep it from hitting the floor. "Thanks." She slipped the cork back into the vial. "Can it be used if we can get it out?"

"I doubt it'd be enough to break the chains. Only enough to let him know we'd attempted to rescue Jaxson," Caidon said. "And what little is left in the vials will evaporate in a day or two. There isn't enough there to keep it from disappearing."

"How do we find another dream weaver?" Elsie slipped the vials back into her pocket. "One who won't be expecting us to come after their magic."

Caidon kept hold of her hand, taking his sister's hand that she held between the bars. "I need to take my sister home before we work on any other plans." He faced Autumn. "Can you picture my home? I need to go there first."

"I'll try." Autumn closed her eyes. "I can see it now."

A leaf formed between Caidon and Elsie's hands and he crushed it between them. The world shimmered and reformed as a forest, Autumn no longer behind bars. "Autumn." His voice was filled with exasperation as he faced his sister, keeping his hold on Elsie.

"I'm sorry. I really did picture your home for a moment, but it's been so long since I visited mine," Autumn said.

He took hold of her hand again. "Try to hold the image for more than a few seconds."

Autumn took a step away from him, slipping out of his grip. "But I'm home. Why can't you picture your place yourself?"

"Because I'm bound to return to the dream weaver for the next decade. I've only been able to travel with my magic because I drained off so much and Elsie has been the one picturing the places. But she's never been to my home. You have." He continued to hold out his hand. "Now picture my home and then I can return you here once we're finished over there."

Autumn pressed her hands against her stomach. "You're his for the next decade? Caidon! I never meant for that to happen."

He took one of her hands from her stomach, smiling briefly. "I know. And I'll figure something out. But first, we need to make sure everyone is safe. Including Jaxson."

"Will you bring him to me when you get him out of there? And give him some of your magic."

"If you want," Caidon said.

Chapter Nineteen

Elsie had been studying the forest while the siblings spoke. "Where are the homes? If this is where you live, where do you actually sleep?" All she could see were trees that were well spaced apart with filtered sunlight reaching the forest floor. It reminded her of the forest in her dream.

Autumn pointed to a nearby tree, the trunk straight and tall. "That's my home. That tree." She made a sweeping gesture. "These are the homes of my friends and family. Other Dryads."

Elsie examined the tree. "There's no door. How do you get inside it?"

Autumn laughed. "I need no door to enter my tree. I just slip inside."

Caidon took a step towards his sister. "Now, please, Autumn. We don't have time for this. It's getting harder to stay awake and harder to fight against going to him."

"What if I take you to our father instead?" Autumn asked. "How are you meant to escape the dream weaver without help?"

Caidon glanced at Elsie. "I have help. We just need you to show her what my home looks like so she can take us there if we need to go there for any reason."

"I hope she can help you." Autumn closed her eyes, the tone of her voice letting Elsie know she had her doubts. "I'm ready."

It took four attempts before Autumn could lead them away from her home, Caidon losing patience with her at one stage. They finally stood out in front of a small manor house made of smooth stone and deep-set timber edged windows.

Caidon faced Elsie. "Memorise this place. I may need your help returning here."

She nodded, her gaze roaming the building. "This is your place?" When he nodded, she asked, "You actually own this?"

"My father gave it to me when I turned eighteen." Caidon continued to hold both their hands. "Let me know when we can leave. Autumn obviously wants to return home."

"I'll be lucky to get a car when I turn eighteen." Elsie took one last look at the place, memorising it. "I'm ready to go."

"Finally," Autumn said. "I'm picturing my home now."

Elsie was tempted to point out it was just about all the Dryad could picture. She remained silent, certain Autumn had been through more than enough.

They returned to the forest and Caidon hugged his sister before she slipped inside a tree. Elsie stared at the rough bark, wanting to run her hands over it to see if there was some sort of opening, but didn't know if she should. It seemed kind of rude to touch a tree someone lived in.

"Can you picture your home?" Caidon asked.

She grinned up at him. "I could even picture Autumn's home." Especially with the amount of times they'd ended up back here.

He chuckled, slipping an arm around her waist. "Then tell me when you can picture your home before I'm too exhausted to take us anywhere else."

She did as he said, letting him know the moment she was picturing it. She felt him sway against her as they arrived in her room. "Are you okay? You can sleep on my bed if you want."

"I can't let myself sleep. He'll find me if I do and order me to return. And more than likely order me to bring you to him. I can't ignore a direct order from him. It's hard enough staying away for now. I'll be lucky if I can stay awake another twenty-four hours. After that, you're on your own. We need to come up with a plan before then."

She wanted to protest. Wanted to beg him to tell her he'd remain at her side until they'd sorted everything out. "What do we do next?"

He shrugged. "Maybe Harold knows where other dream weavers live."

"I doubt he'd tell us." She spun at the sound of her bedroom door opening.

Marinda stopped in the doorway. "Your mum just left. You can't imagine how much of an effort it was to keep her from checking on you. I had to convince her you'd barely slept and had just fallen asleep again and shouldn't be woken. That even I wasn't going back into the bedroom until you woke so I didn't risk disturbing you. I had to promise to get you to call the moment you did wake." She glanced around the room. "Where is Jaxson?"

Elsie tried to think of a way to explain what had happened. She was certain Marinda wouldn't blame her for not trying hard enough to convince Jaxson to go with them. She hadn't tried because she'd known there was no way she could convince him and wasting time arguing would have risked them all being caught.

"Jaxson refused to be rescued while Autumn remained behind," Caidon said.

"That's so typical of him." Marinda sighed heavily. "Now what? I take it he's still a prisoner."

"It's a little more than the typical reason," Elsie said.

"What do you mean?" Marinda asked.

"I think he's in love with Caidon's sister. The Dryad. He didn't exactly say he was, but the way he talked about her, and looked at her, and what he did say makes me think he is."

Marinda stared open-mouthed at Elsie, eventually bursting into laughter. "Guess you don't have to worry about ditching him now."

Elsie's lips briefly curved into a wry smile. "I broke up with him through a text. Remember?"

"Oh, yeah. I forgot about that after all that's happened. What–"

Caidon interrupted Marinda. "We're running out of time. We need to find two more dream weavers before I lose the fight against this promise."

"Caidon…" Elsie's voice trailed off at the strain and exhaustion she saw on his face. She reached for him.

He captured her hand between his. "I'll be fine as long as we sort this out quickly."

"How are we meant to find two more dream weavers?" Marinda asked.

Elsie shrugged, then drew out of Caidon's grip. "Where's my phone?"

Marinda pointed towards the set of drawers. "What do you need it for? It isn't like dream weavers would have a phone you can call them on."

Elsie called her father, listening to the ring tone. "No, but my father might know other dream weavers. After all, spinners end up taking things to them and he's moved around a bit over the years so he might have met a few. Well, kind of met them in a sleep type of fashion." When the call rang out, she pressed the button to call him again.

After four attempts, she set the phone down with a growl. "Of course he's not there when I need him."

"He might have killed himself white water rafting." Marinda frowned. "Or would you call it white water surfing?"

"I doubt it. He'll probably be around longer than most with how ridiculously lucky he is when it comes to getting away with doing stupid things." Elsie turned her back on her phone, running her fingers over the pebble in her pocket. "I didn't want to ask Harold. That doesn't seem like a good idea after what he said."

Caidon drew her hand away from her pocket. "I can take us there if you can picture it rather than waste the pebble. You might need it for another day."

She tried not to think about the day he referred to. A day when he could no longer use his magic to take her places because he was completely under the control of the dream weaver. "Okay. Let me put it somewhere safe first." She put the pebble, along with the two vials that had contained dream weaver magic, in the top drawer of the set of drawers, nestling everything amongst the underwear she kept in there.

Caidon held out the three vials of his magic. "Can you put them in there too? I'd rather not keep carrying them around with me."

She put them in the drawer and closed it, leaning against the set of drawers as she faced him. "Would it help draining off more magic?"

He shook his head. "I have so little of it as it is. Removing more won't make any difference." He held out his hand. "Are you ready to see Harold?"

She wasn't in the slightest, but placed her hand in his anyway.

Marinda hurried forward. "What about me? Can I go with you too?"

"No. You need to stay here and keep my mum from finding out what's going on. I don't want her involved." Elsie looked up at Caidon. "I can picture my great grandfather's dump."

They left to the sound of Marinda's laughter, the world reforming around them in towering piles of items. Harold came striding towards them, a scowl on his face.

Elsie drew away from Caidon, quickly speaking before Harold could. "If you won't give me two more drops of dream weaver magic, then at least tell me where I can find two others that I can get magic from."

"I owe you nothing. Do you hear? You're as demanding as your father. I gave you more than what you were entitled to and still you pester me." Harold glared at her.

She took a stumbling step back from the anger in his voice. "My friend has been taken-"

"I don't care if your entire family are in danger or that useless father of yours is dying. I am not your personal servant to run around after you and grant you your every wish," Harold stated. "Don't bother visiting me again. I have more than enough useless people left here for me to deal with by dream spinners. I don't need more of them in my life."

"You kill them?" Elsie demanded. "The ones they leave behind, you drain them of magic and kill them?"

"What do you think I am? Some monster to kill what was once my kind? I haven't lost all touch with my humanity yet. Maybe one day soon. Probably far too soon if I keep getting pestered by the family I left behind." Harold looked at her pointedly.

"I just need help one more-"

Harold interrupted Elsie. "It's always one more time. Always. Ron says that to me constantly."

Her hands tightened into fists as she stepped away from Caidon, taking several steps closer to Harold. "I'm not like my father. I never have been."

"You could have fooled me from where I'm standing." Harold glanced at Caidon. "I will assume you have your own way to return home and don't need any of my help with that either."

Chapter Twenty

Elsie pressed her lips together on all the demands she wanted to make. About to turn away, she took another step towards Harold instead. "I think you have lost touch with your humanity. Not killing the dream spinners proves nothing. It costs you nothing. This is what being human is about. Putting yourself out for someone with no gain for yourself. You're not even slightly human anymore." She turned her back on him and moved close to Caidon, taking his hand to look up at him. "Take me home." She pictured her bedroom as she said the words.

They left before Harold had the chance to speak again, Marinda rushing towards them as they arrived in the bedroom. She grabbed hold of their hands. "Did he help you?"

Elsie shook her head, trying not to think about how badly she needed sleep.

"What do we do now?" Marinda asked.

Elsie shrugged. She didn't have a clue. Before she could speak the words aloud, her phone rang, causing her to jump. She looked at the screen. It was her father. "Yeah?"

"You rang, sweetheart?"

"Yeah."

"Did you want something?"

"I need to find a couple of dream weavers that I can take magic from," Elsie said.

There was a moment of silence before Ron replied. "You're going to steal their magic?"

"Well, I can't exactly afford to buy it and I get the impression most of them don't sell straight dream weaver magic anyway, only magic altered by theirs."

"I might know someone who can tell us where one dream weaver is. This sounds like a blast. When do you want to go?" Ron asked.

"Hang on a minute. You weren't invited. I just need to know where to find a dream weaver," Elsie said.

Again there was a moment of silence before Ron spoke. "You expect me to provide the information and not join in on the fun."

She automatically nodded, even though he couldn't see her. "Yeah. That's about it."

"Why would I do that?" Ron demanded.

"Maybe because you're my father," Elsie suggested.

"You sound like your mum," Ron accused.

"So you keep telling me." She thought it best not to insult him by saying she preferred to be like her mum than like him.

He sighed heavily. "I suppose I probably should see what I can do. This father business isn't as interesting as I thought it might be."

"Funny thing, that," Elsie said dryly.

"I'll let you know what I find out." Ron disconnected the call before Elsie could reply.

She slipped her phone into a pocket of her jeans, looking from Caidon to Marinda, who were both focused on her. "He might be able to help us with the location of a dream weaver. He's ringing back."

"When?" Marinda asked. "It won't be like some of the previous times where you've waited days for him to get back to you, will it?"

"It better not. I'll give him a few hours then start pestering him if he hasn't called," Elsie said.

"What do we do while we wait?" Marinda asked.

Caidon headed for the bedroom door. "Keep moving so we don't fall asleep."

Elsie paced the house with him, regularly checking the time on her phone. In the end she set an alarm to go off four hours after her initial call to her father, thinking that was more than enough time for him to get the information.

After she stopped checking her phone so much, Elsie lost track of time as they paced the house, having no idea how many hours it had been since the call when she stumbled, nearly tripping over her own feet.

Caidon caught her to him, wrapping his arms around her as he leaned against the hallway wall. "Are you fine?"

"I need to sit down. Just for a few minutes. Or I'm likely to fall over," Elsie said.

"We can't risk it." Caidon remained leaning against the wall, his eyes closed.

She rested her head on his chest, fighting back a yawn. She couldn't prevent it. "I wish he'd hurry and ring. He better not take days to get the information."

"We don't have days. Should you ring him back and let him know that?" His arms tensed around her. "I can feel the promise trying to force me to return to the dream weaver. I might have another five hours before I can no longer keep myself from obeying."

Fear raced through her and she tightened her arms around his waist. "You can't go back to him. There has to be something we can do to stop you."

"Tie me to a chair and keep my hands immobile so I can't crush a leaf in them," Caidon suggested.

"That sounds like a terrible idea." Her ear was pressed against his chest and she listened to his heart, the steady beat making her eyes slowly close.

"Hmm."

"There has to be a better idea than that." Her words were slow and the few seconds of wakefulness the fear had given her faded as exhaustion again tugged at her.

"Hmm."

She sank more heavily against him, wondering where Marinda was. Had she left? That didn't seem likely. But she hadn't seen her on their last circuit around the house. Her body felt heavy and Caidon's arms around her were warm, supporting her as she sank even more against him.

"I knew it was only time."

Elsie drew out of Caidon's arms to face the dream weaver. It took her a few seconds to realise she was dreaming, Caidon beside her in the dream, the familiar sight of the hallway having confused her for a moment.

Caidon stepped around Elsie, standing between her and the dream weaver. "I would make another bargain with you."

"I have your next decade. What more do you have to offer?" the dream weaver demanded.

"How about the decade after that if you leave the dream spinner alone?" Caidon asked.

"No!" Elsie stepped around him to clamp her hand over his mouth. "No. I don't agree and I'd never forgive you if you did that."

Caidon drew her hand from his mouth, his grip tight around her wrist when she tried to prevent him. "You have no say in this bargain."

"You do that and I won't leave him alone," Elsie warned. "Your deal would be for nothing."

"It isn't an equal trade," the dream weaver said. "I'd want three decades."

Elsie struggled to break free of Caidon's grip, shaking her head when he opened his mouth. Not knowing what else to do to keep him from saying anything, she rose onto the tips of her toes and pressed her lips against his.

He returned the kiss for a moment, before drawing back, his lips curving into a smile. He glanced past her to the dream weaver. "No deal."

"Then you have nothing to offer me," the dream weaver said. "Return to my place and bring the dream spinner with you."

Caidon took a step back from her, running into the wall of the hallway. "I'm sorry." He vanished.

"No." She took a step forward, her hand stretched out to the place where he'd been. She spun to face the dream weaver. "What have you done with him?"

The dream weaver's lips twisted into a smile. "Nothing. Yet. But you owe me for the two you stole from me. And I will start with the boy you brought to me."

"Don't you dare hurt Jaxson." She took a threatening step towards the dream weaver.

He laughed. "I have nothing to fear from you. This very moment Caidon will be collecting your sleeping body and bringing it back to me. Then we'll see how little power you truly have." He vanished before she could speak.

She stared at where he'd been before moving forward, shaking her head. "No. Come back. I wasn't finished talking to you." Maybe she could have made a deal with him. No one answered. She was alone. And she had to wake up. Before Caidon could take her back to the dream weaver. There'd be no chance to make a bargain then.

She pinched herself. It hurt, like she was already awake. Telling herself to wake up didn't help either. Nor did lightly slapping her cheeks. How deeply was she asleep? Was it already too late? Would she wake to find herself in a cage?

A piercing sound could be heard in the distance, slowly becoming louder. Then she was aware of Marinda calling her name. She woke, slumped against the wall on the hallway floor, Marinda trying to drag Caidon back from her, the alarm on the phone going off. She stumbled to her feet, lowering her head and barrelling into Caidon, wincing when he groaned at the impact.

He landed hard on the floor, looking up at Elsie. "I'm sorry. I can't disobey him." He struggled to rise.

Elsie grabbed Marinda's hand, dragging her friend with her towards her bedroom. Behind her she heard Caidon stumble and catch himself with the help of the wall. How tired he was might be their only advantage, but she wasn't far off being just as tired as him. The little sleep she'd had the first time she'd encountered the dream weaver in her dreams wasn't much more than Caidon had slept.

Marinda slammed the door behind them, leaning against it. "What happened? Why's he trying to take you from here? And why did he yell out to me that he's taking you to the dream weaver?"

Elsie locked the door and leaned against it beside Marinda. "So you could stop him. He doesn't have a choice. We fell asleep and the dream weaver invaded our dreams. He ordered Caidon to return to him and bring me too."

The door shuddered. Marinda squealed. "I don't think it'll hold long against him. What are we going to do now?"

She fumbled for her phone, keeping her back pressed against the door, wincing as it shuddered again. She called her father, speaking the moment he picked up. "Do you know how to teach someone how to use magic to travel to places?"

"Nah, I don't hang out with Fae and I was never interested in getting any of their magic. What have you done?"

"Nothing." He didn't deserve being told all that had happened. Her mum was right. She didn't really have a father. "Call me when you find out where there's a dream weaver."

"Sure. I'm waiting to hear back from my mate. In the meantime, I'm off to the Gold Coast. Got a friend thinking of building a rocket-propelled car. It should be a blast. If he can get the thing built."

She started to demand if he was deliberately trying to kill himself, but ended up keeping the words to herself. If anything, he'd probably survive while his friend died. "I'll talk to you later." She waited for his reply before she hung up, turning to Marinda, pressing her shoulder against the shuddering door. "Sorry. It looks like we're on our own."

"I don't think we're going to keep him out of here much longer."

The door shuddered again and then there was silence. Elsie lay down on the floor and peered under the door. She couldn't see him. Was he waiting out of sight in an effort to lure them out?

"What about your grandfather?" Marinda asked.

"He said I was never to visit him again." She rose to her feet, staring at the door handle, not sure if she should open it and check the hallway.

"We can use the pebble to go to his place and from there go somewhere else. Find someone who can teach me how to use magic," Marinda suggested. "Surely there's someone who'll be willing to help us."

"Get ready to slam the door shut. I'm having a look." She rested her hand on the door handle.

Marinda took a step back. "Are you sure that's a good idea?"

"Probably not, but I doubt he's given up. Not while he's under orders to the dream weaver." She pulled the door open, looking in both directions. The hallway was empty.

Chapter Twenty-One

Elsie realised instantly what Caidon was planning. "He's going to come in the window." She raced to the set of drawers, grabbing the pebble along with the two empty vials and three full ones. She shoved the vials in her pockets. The sound of breaking glass had her spinning to face the window. Her bed was covered in glass shards.

Marinda joined her by the set of drawers, grabbing hold of her hand. "Better do something quickly."

Elsie dropped the pebble onto the floor as Caidon entered the broken window, a shard of glass cutting his arm and causing blood to drip onto the bed. She stomped onto the pebble as he broke into a run, landing on the floor as the world shimmered and reformed.

Marinda clung to Elsie's hand. "Can he follow us?"

"He knows this location and he's been ordered to bring me back." She scanned the area, not able to see much with all the towering piles of items that surrounded them.

"We should get out of here. He could be around any corner, laying in wait for us," Marinda said.

"I have no idea which direction to go in." Elsie took a hesitant step forward.

Harold stepped out from behind a pile of lost items to block their way. "I knew you'd be back. You lot always are."

She stepped in front of Marinda, who still clung to her hand, drawing out of her friend's tight grip, not sure what Harold was likely to do to them for trespassing. "I didn't plan to see you. We just needed a way back to the realms of the Fae and this was the only way we knew." As well as needing a quick exit from her house. But she wasn't about to tell him anything more than necessary. "If you get out of the way, we'll find someone who can teach us how to travel using magic."

"Anyone you ask will expect you to pay a steep price," Harold warned. "I live on the edge of the Fringes where the worst of this realm live."

Elsie looked him up and down. "Really. That doesn't surprise me at all."

Harold laughed, a deep, rolling sound that didn't match his gangly figure. "Maybe you aren't so bad after all. At least you're more entertaining than Ron."

"I don't plan to stay and chat. I'm rapidly running out of time." Elsie had no idea when the dream weaver would take the magic from Jaxson, but she didn't want to risk being too late to save him. "Can you get out of my way? I need to find the exit to this place."

"Then you're going in the wrong direction." Harold gestured behind her. "It's that way."

Grabbing hold of Marinda's arm, Elsie headed in the opposite direction. She stopped when Harold appeared in front of her. A glance behind showed it must be him because he was no longer standing where she'd left him. "What do you want?"

"What is going on? Where is the Fae you were with earlier? Why do you need to learn how to use magic to travel to places? Neither of you have any magic."

Elsie couldn't get past Harold. He'd chosen to stand where the path between the towering piles narrowed. "I thought you didn't want me to hang around here. I can't exactly leave if you're in the way."

Harold remained where he was. "You were the one who turned up on my property like it was some path you're welcome to use as you please."

"We need to find someone who can help us," Marinda insisted. "We're wasting time. Jaxson could be dying."

Elsie held Harold's gaze with her own. "I'm trying to save my friend. The one you weren't willing to help me with. Unless you've suddenly decided you want to give me two drops of dream weaver magic and transport us to where Jaxson is being held, then get out of our way so we can find someone who can help."

Harold looked her up and down. "I think I like you a lot better than Ron." He tossed a pebble in the air towards her. "Drop in and visit some time. Tell me how it went. I'm intrigued to know if you save him. I doubt Ron has ever put himself out this much for another human in his entire life." He brushed past her and headed back in the direction he'd come from.

"You-" Elsie drew back a hand, planning to throw the pebble at him.

Marinda grabbed hold of her hand, preventing her from throwing it. "We might need it." Marinda grinned. "Even if it's only to come back and abuse him for being so pathetic."

Elsie breathed in deeply and slowly released her breath. "You're right. He just annoys me. There's no reason why he can't help." She slipped the pebble into her pocket before heading in the direction Harold had indicated was the exit.

It took them several attempts to find the exit, becoming lost in the maze that was Harold's property. Elsie was tempted to go with Marinda's suggestion of pushing through the towering piles, but worried they'd collapse on them rather than away from them. She really didn't care how Harold would have felt about her knocking them over after he'd refused to help.

Stepping past the outer pile, they spotted a tall timber fence that separated them from a ramshackle tumble of buildings. Elsie stopped in the open gateway, not sure it was a good idea to enter what looked like it was probably some sort of slum town.

Marinda grabbed hold of Elsie's arm, pressing herself against her friend's side. "Do you think we should go out there? It doesn't look very safe."

"You can stay here if you want," Elsie reluctantly suggested.

"But I'm the one planning to have magic. Shouldn't I be the one asking for help?" Marinda's grip on Elsie's arm tightened.

"When are you going to have it?" Elsie asked.

"I don't know. Do you think I should have it first?" Marinda looked from Harold's property to the town. "Maybe we should try asking him again for help."

"It'd be a waste of time. And we don't know how much time Jaxson has left." Elsie took a step forward, Marinda moving with her.

Marinda let go with one hand and took the vial of magic out of her pocket. She studied the contents. "What if I can't figure out how to use it?"

"Then we come up with another plan," Elsie assured her.

Marinda released Elsie's arm and held out her hand so she could tip the contents of the vial onto it. The magic sat on her palm for a moment, then it sank into her skin. "That feels weird." She returned the vial to her pocket, then brushed the tips of her fingers across her palm that was now empty. "How odd." She looked up at Elsie. "Now what?"

Elsie linked her arm with Marinda's. "I guess we find someone to teach you how to use it." She took another deep breath before she entered the street in front of them. It was made of broken cobblestones, more missing than were actually in place.

"What if we get lost?" Marinda asked.

"We just need to remember each direction we take."

"We could always turn left," Marinda suggested.

"Then we'd be doing circles." Elsie went straight ahead, ignoring the turns she could take in each direction.

"Do you think only going straight ahead is a good idea?" Marinda moved closer to Elsie, looking in every direction.

Elsie had no clue what was a good idea. She shrugged in answer, continuing along the same street. "I think the town looks a little better ahead of us. Less run down."

"Are you sure that isn't wishful thinking?" Marinda asked.

Elsie shrugged, remaining on the street that, although it mostly went straight ahead, had some twists and turns in it at various points. Eventually, they reached a 'T' intersection and Elsie turned left, hearing music coming from that direction.

Over her initial fear, Marinda examined everything they passed, including the handful of people, some who looked more animal than human. She kept her voice low as she exclaimed excitedly about everything. Her mouth rounded in surprise as the two of them entered an area filled with a medieval-looking market. She grabbed hold of Elsie. "I don't think I ever want to go home. Look at this place."

Stalls were scattered around the outside, including rickety tables displaying wares. Shops were open with inexpertly painted signs proclaiming their names, and street performers entertained the people who filled the area haggling, drinking, eating, laughing, gambling, talking and fighting.

"Surely we can find someone in here to teach me," Marinda said.

"I can teach you many things," a voice said from behind them.

They spun to see two Fae metres from them, the younger male grinning. Elsie didn't know if she should make the cutting reply that instantly came to mind or back away and lose themselves in the crowd. Caidon was faster and stronger than her so these two were likely to be as well.

"All sorts of things." The younger one continued to grin.

Marinda raised her chin. "I'm only interested in learning one thing. And that's how to travel around using magic."

The older Fae took a step forward. "Not all who attempt to learn that are capable of doing so."

Elsie met Marinda's gaze, shrugging slightly at the questioning look. She had no idea how magic worked and she was pretty sure the way the Fae had worded the information meant it was the truth.

"What would you offer in return?" the older Fae asked.

"What I want to know is who owns you. I'd make an offer to take you off their hands," the younger Fae said.

"No one–"

Elsie stepped back on Marinda's foot to interrupt her protests. Neither of them knew how things worked here. What if it was normal for humans to be owned by Fae? From the way the younger one had spoken, it had sounded that way. "We have a vial of magic we can trade."

"Neither of us have any need of more magic, but the magic collector might be interested," the older Fae said.

"What about a dream catcher? Do you know where we can find one of them?" Marinda asked.

"There's Harold out near the deserted section of the Fringes," the older Fae said.

"What do you want with a dream catcher?" the younger Fae demanded. "Most of them are insane. All that un-processed magic lying around interfering with their heads."

"It's the noise of all the unprocessed magic that effects them," the older Fae corrected.

"Exactly. Interferes with their heads," the younger Fae said.

The older Fae slowly shook his head. "I don't think you understand the mechanics of it."

The younger Fae shrugged. "It doesn't matter. No one goes near a dream weaver unless they absolutely have to or are desperate. Look how the Fringes have slowly cleared out over near Harold. No one even wants to live near one."

"It's all that unprocessed magic he has lying around. They can feel the pressure of it," the older Fae said.

The younger Fae stepped around his companion, looking Marinda and Elsie up and down. "I don't think either of you are owned by Fae. I think you're mine for the taking."

Chapter Twenty-Two

Fear exploded through Elsie and she struggled to remain where she was rather than run from the Fae. She doubted running would help. He'd soon catch up with them without any effort. "Caidon."

"Who?" the younger Fae demanded.

"His sister is a Dryad," Marinda said.

The younger Fae grinned. "He's no threat to me."

"What about his father?" Elsie asked.

The younger Fae's grin vanished. "Are you the son's or the father's pet?"

"Would it make a difference if the father was the one who gave us to the son?" Marinda asked.

"You don't want that kind of trouble," the older Fae warned.

Elsie somehow remained calm, her entire body feeling like it was poised to run. "There are dream weavers in my family too." She smiled briefly. "I'm sure you don't want that kind of trouble either."

The younger Fae glared at her. "Then why do you need to find another dream weaver if you have family you can approach?"

"Because family don't always agree with what I want to do," Elsie said.

The younger Fae glanced at the older Fae. "Everyone has that problem at various times."

She managed not to grin at the sight of his disgruntled expression. "Do you know any other than Harold?"

"There's one who lives off in the forest in that direction." The older Fae nodded in a direction that was over his shoulder.

"Does that one have a name?" Elsie asked.

The older Fae shook his head. "He lives in a fortified dwelling about a day's travel from here."

Elsie's heart sank. "In a forest that grows close to his house that has a tower on one side of it?"

The older Fae inclined his head. "That would be the one." He took a step to the side. "I have things to buy at the courtyard markets. If you will excuse me."

Elsie wanted to protest. What if he was all that was keeping the young Fae in his place?

"Where is the magic collector?" Marinda asked.

The older Fae gave brief directions before he inclined his head and strode away. He was soon lost from sight in the crowd.

The younger Fae remained with them, eyeing Marinda. "Are you both owned by Caidon?"

"You don't need to go shopping in the courtyard markets too?" Elsie asked.

"I have better things to do than shop." He moved closer to Marinda, who kept glancing at Elsie.

She took Marinda's hand, determined not to get anyone killed. Not Jaxson, and not the two of them. "Then we'll leave you to them since you don't seem to know the location of any other dream weavers."

"It's not like they're common or that there are a lot of them," the younger Fae protested.

Elsie took a step backwards, drawing Marinda with her. "I'm sure we've taken up enough of your time."

The younger Fae's lips slowly curved into a smile. "Now that I think of it, I doubt there's anyone around here who'd run to Caidon with stories of what I might have done."

Elsie backed away further, squeezing Marinda's arm when she started to speak. "There are always people willing to tell tales."

He advanced on them. "Only if there's a benefit to them."

She continued to retreat. "When rewards are given for tales told, there are those who'd talk a great deal."

"Some things are worth the risk." He darted forward, grabbing Marinda's arm and dragging her away from Elsie's side.

She held on tight, worried what would happen if he managed to pull Marinda from her. "Let go."

He held on. "I don't think Caidon is as interested in the two of you as you make out. Otherwise why would you be here on your own?"

"Trying to learn something he doesn't think we need to know while he's away for the day." Elsie held on tight, Marinda struggling to free her arm.

"I'm sure I could beat him in a fight. After all, from what I can recall of him, he's a couple of decades younger than me and has limited experience in combat."

Marinda stepped forward in a rush, stomping on the Fae's foot. When he let her go, she spun, heading for the crowd in the courtyard markets, dragging Elsie with her. "Maybe getting magic wasn't such a great idea. There was hardly anything it'd let me say. Having to stick with telling the truth is harder than I thought it'd be."

Elsie stayed close to Miranda, dodging people as they ran as fast as possible through the crowd. "Being able to lie didn't help me much. I had no idea what to say to him half the time and the other half I kept expecting him to call out 'liar' and demand we tell him the real truth." She tugged Marinda down one of the alleys leading off the courtyard.

"Where are we going?" Marinda asked.

"To find the magic collector. Maybe he'll know someone who can teach you how to use your magic." She dodged and weaved through the crowd, unable to go as fast as she'd have liked. A glance over her shoulder showed they weren't followed. She didn't know if he'd tried and lost them or hadn't bothered once they'd run from him. She slowed, making it easier to navigate through the crowd.

"What if I can't use it? The older one said not everyone can," Marinda said.

"Does that mean you don't want to try?"

"Of course it doesn't. I'm just worried it won't help."

"Then we'll do something else." Elsie came to a stop, drawing Marinda to a stop with her amongst the thinning crowd. The younger Fae hadn't given up. He'd figured out where they were going and waited ahead for them. Just past the crowd in a street they needed to turn down.

"What's wrong n–" Marinda broke off mid-word. "Oh."

"We could go back to Harold's and wait until dark before we try and sneak over here," Elsie suggested.

"I'd rather stay in the creepy deserted area outside of Harold's than be caught by that Fae." Marinda shuddered. "I dread to think what he has planned for me."

A woman walking past gave them a second look, coming to a stop to look them up and down. "Very pretty. Are you both here with someone?"

They answered together. "Yes."

Elsie grinned. "Sorry." She turned her back on the woman, heading back in the direction they'd come from.

Marinda didn't speak until they were back at Harold's entrance gates. "I was worried I wouldn't have been able to say yes to that woman. But I guess humans count when asked a non-specific question like that." She nodded towards the gates. "Are we going in there?"

"I don't know." Elsie glanced over her shoulder. The area of the town behind them remained empty.

"We could find a quiet corner to have a rest in," Marinda suggested.

"I can't sleep, remember?"

"Oh. Yeah. I forgot." Marinda sighed. "We're not very good at this."

"We haven't exactly had to do anything like this before." Hearing a noise, Elsie glanced over her shoulder. Her mouth dropped open when she saw Caidon strode towards them. He still looked exhausted, so she assumed he hadn't had a chance to rest either.

Marinda groaned. "This is getting ridiculous. It feels like everyone's out to get us."

"Not everyone, but more than enough to make it a problem." Elsie backed away. "You run, I'll distract him."

"Elsie-"

Caidon called out, interrupting Marinda's protests. "He told me that if you didn't come quietly, I was to go after someone important to you. Like Marinda or your mother."

She momentarily closed her eyes, swaying on the spot as she fought the fear and exhaustion that washed over her. She only knew of two dream weavers. And she didn't have time to wait for her father to get back to her. She leaned towards Marinda, lowering her voice. "Ask Harold to send you home." She started towards Caidon.

Marinda grabbed hold of her, halting her progress. "Are you crazy? The dream weaver will kill you."

"I'm not about to let him go after my mum. Or you." She pulled out of Marinda's grip and ran to meet Caidon, ignoring Marinda's demands for her to come back.

Caidon wrapped his arms around her as she reached him. "I have no choice."

She slid her arms around his waist, resting her head on his shoulder. "I know. I don't blame you for this."

"He's not the sort to play fair," Caidon warned.

Hearing Marinda call out to her, Elsie raised her head and met Caidon's gaze. "Get us out of here before Marinda does something stupid."

He gave a single nod before he formed a leaf and transported them to the dream weaver's kitchen. They were in front of the open trapdoor. "I'm so sorry, Elsie."

"I know." She let him lead her down the stairs, wanting to make sure Jaxson still lived. The relief at spotting him leaning against the bars of the cage made her feel shaky and she stumbled against Caidon.

"Are you fine?"

Before she could tell Caidon she wasn't in the slightest bit fine, Jaxson spoke.

"You've come back for me?" He struggled to rise. "Is Autumn okay? Did you manage to take her home? Is she safe?"

"Autumn is safe." Elsie wished she could tell Jaxson she'd come back for him.

"I can't put you in a cage next to him," Caidon said. "I was ordered not to."

Jaxson stilled. "Is something wrong?"

"You look no worse." She still couldn't bring herself to tell him the bad news.

"He's taken no more magic from me since you left." Jaxson looked from one to the other. "What is happening?"

Caidon opened the door to the cage opposite Jaxson. "I really am sorry. You can't imagine how difficult it is for me to imprison you."

She leaned forward, lightly brushing her lips across his. "Same."

He frowned. Before he could say anything, Elsie pushed him into the cage and slammed the door shut, turning the key in the lock. He stumbled backwards, quickly regaining his balance. "It won't help, Elsie." The smell of his magic filled the room.

Chapter Twenty-Three

Elsie ran up the stairs and towards the front door. Caidon appeared in front of her as she entered the tower, standing between her and the exit.

"If you run, he'll send me after one of them," Caidon warned.

"Not if you keep looking for me."

"It won't help. You need to come up with a better plan than that."

She was trying to, but she didn't exactly have many options. Breaking into a run, she barrelled into Caidon. He tried to grab hold of her, but he was off balance and stumbled, needing to catch himself before he could do anything about grabbing hold of her.

She burst out the front door, not checking over her shoulder as she ran into the forest. Dawn was breaking, so there were more shadows than light amongst the trees. She tried to move fast, but silently. Glancing over her shoulder, she saw Caidon headed directly towards her. Obviously she wasn't silent enough.

She had no idea what she was doing, making the plan up as she went along. So far, she wasn't doing too great. She needed to get back inside and find a way to set Jaxson free. Maybe if she could take him back to Harold he might remove the chains.

Caidon strode directly towards her. "Come out, Elsie. You're not very quiet."

She slowed, trying to remain silent as she angled around to head into the building. If she could get back inside before him, maybe it'd be possible to lock him outside. At least long enough for her to get Jaxson out of the cage. After that, she didn't know what she'd do. Reaching the edge of the forest, she made a break for it, reaching the front door and slamming it shut behind her. There was a timber bar that slipped into place to lock it.

Caidon slammed against the door, causing it to shudder slightly. Although not as bad as the bedroom door had shuddered. "Locking it won't help."

She didn't stick around to find out what else he had to say since he currently followed the dream weaver's orders. Running along the corridor, she slowed to a stop when she heard voices ahead of her.

"Take the boy to my workroom. I'll take the magic from him while I wait for Caidon to catch the dream spinner," the dream weaver ordered.

She spun, heading for the room with the spiral staircase. Wild plans raced through her mind, none of them in the least bit practical. She had no idea what she'd do when she reached the workroom, but she had to do something. She couldn't let him kill Jaxson.

Arriving in the workroom, she scanned the area. It looked the same as last time, so she hid behind the dollhouse, regretting that choice the moment she'd made it. But it was too late. She heard footsteps coming up the second spiral staircase. Peering through the windows of the dollhouse, she tried to remain silent when she saw two people place Jaxson on the mesh shelf and remove his chains. It took all her willpower to remain where she was rather than race straight out and grab him. There was no way she would have been able to overpower two people and take Jaxson out of there.

The moment they left the room, she started to rise to her feet, quickly crouching back down when the dream weaver entered. Caidon walked behind him. Her breath stopped and she remained frozen behind the dollhouse.

The dream weaver stopped in front of his workbench. "Bring back the girl you told me about. The friend. She'll hand herself over in exchange for the friend. I'm certain of it."

Caidon nodded then vanished, the scent of his magic rapidly fading.

Elsie leaned her head against the dollhouse, closing her eyes as she tried to think what to do. Caidon was going after Marinda, she had no idea where her friend was, the dream weaver was about to drain the magic from Jaxson possibly until he died and she had no way of preventing any of it. She was completely powerless.

Opening her eyes, she peered through one of the upper windows. The dream weaver had begun and a glint of light formed at the point of the mesh. How much longer did Jaxson have? Did he have two or three drops of magic left in him? How long would it take for the magic to be taken out? As long as it had taken to remove it from items?

Her chest felt tight and her breath came fast. She tried to slow it down, realising her heart also raced. A glance around showed nothing she could use as a weapon. Checking again, she saw the drop of magic was increasing at a faster pace than it had for items. Soon it would fall into the vial and the dream weaver might only have one more to take from Jaxson. She couldn't let that happen.

As much as she hated the idea of becoming a dream weaver, it might be her only chance to save everyone. Including herself. Her gaze remained on the drop of magic as she came up in a crouch, ready to dash across the room to take it. The moment it started to fall, she ran towards the workbench, not realising there were guards in the room until she was partway across it. She snatched the vial at the same moment as one of the guards barrelled into her, knocking the vial from her hand. It skittered across the floor and she elbowed the guard in the face as she struggled to escape him.

The dream weaver went for the vial and Elsie threw herself forward, her fingers grazing the vial as it was picked up. She launched upwards, knocking the vial from the dream weaver's hand. It spun towards the floor, both of them going for it as the guard she'd elbowed came after her, the second one close on his heels.

The vial shattered as it hit the floor. Elsie dived for it, pressing her hand against the drop of magic that lay on the floorboards, a sensation of pin pricks grazing her palm. A guard grabbed hold of her and she fought to stay where she was, feeling a piece of glass cut her hand. He drew her away from the floor and she scanned the area for the magic. It was gone, yet she felt no different. She frowned. Or did she? How was she meant to know what magic felt like?

"Let her go. It's too late," the dream weaver said. "I guess I'll have to make do with the friends in exchange for what I would have taken from her." His lips twisted into a smile.

"No. You can't have them." She fought to escape the guard's grip, stumbling when he let her go. "They're my friends. I'm not about to desert them."

"What will you offer in exchange for them?" the dream weaver demanded.

"Marinda isn't yours. I never brought her to you," Elsie stated.

"The boy is mine, though. You brought him to me."

She couldn't exactly argue that comment even though she really wanted to. "It wasn't him I wanted to be rid of. It was our relationship. You can have the relationship, not the person."

"That is impossible. You can't take magic from something intangible," the dream weaver said.

"If that is all he is to you, another drop of magic, then what if I give one to you?"

"You owe me more than a single drop of magic. You stole two others from me and two drops of magic." He looked her up and down. "On second thought, I don't think you deserve to take back something you threw away."

A crashing sound had them both spinning towards the workbench. Jaxson rolled off the bench top and onto the floor, trying to land on his feet. He failed, lying sprawled on the floor instead. He raised his head. "Don't, Elsie. I'm not worth you becoming a slave to him. He treats those who work for him badly."

Elsie crouched beside Jaxson, helping him to his feet. He felt strange to her touch, like static electricity. "What's wrong with him?"

"You can feel it already?" the dream weaver asked. "The magic in him waiting to be collected."

She let go of Jaxson, backing away from him, clasping her hands together rather than reach for him when he swayed on his feet.

The dream weaver laughed. "It takes more than touch to remove it. You need to draw it from him."

"I don't want to take any from him." She frowned, the entire room feeling like it had a hum to it, the noise steadily increasing. "You have cicadas in here?"

"It's the magic. It will drive you crazy if you let it keep building," the dream weaver said. "Yet drawing it off is equally as damaging to you. Stay and do my work for me. Give me a decade and I'll give you your friend and accept it as payment for all you've stolen from me."

"No." The word burst from her. "A decade is too long."

"A decade isn't that long considering how long you'll live. You owe me. Theft should be punished."

"You stole my friend."

"I know you believe that, obviously since you can't lie anymore, but that isn't the way things work."

"You don't have to take the magic from people. That isn't necessary. Not all dream weavers do."

"I prefer to keep my sanity rather than risk it by letting any of the items go. That includes any living thing brought here by dream spinners. Even their pets."

She stared at him, open-mouthed. It took her a moment before she could speak. "You kill innocent pets?"

He shrugged. "Dream spinners shouldn't get something they don't want."

"We don't know what will happen. Do you think we want to leave things with you? We should be told what might happen. It isn't fair to expect us to follow particular rules when we don't even know of their existence." She slipped an arm around Jaxson's waist when he looked like he might collapse.

The dream weaver laughed. "Do you really think life is meant to be fair?"

She opened her mouth again to argue, closing it instead. They needed to get out of here and find Marinda. What if she hadn't been able to convince Harold to take her home? Thoughts of Harold reminded her of the pebble. She had her way out of here. Backing away from the dream weaver, she slid a hand in her pocket, keeping her other arm around Jaxson. "Offer me a better bargain and I'll consider it. The current one isn't fair. And before you tell me again that life isn't fair, that doesn't mean I'm about to accept bargains that aren't."

"I have no reason to reduce my offer. You're the one in need here, not me." The dream weaver remained where he was.

"That's where you're wrong. I have other options." She dropped the pebble onto the floor, stomping on it. The world shimmered, before the dream weaver could take more than a step forward, and reformed. She winced at the high-pitched sound filling the area around her. It was like thousands of cicadas all calling out at once. How could Harold stand it?

"Where are we?" Jaxson eyed the tower of items they stood beside.

"My great grandfather's place." She scanned the area. No one was in sight. "Marinda!"

"You don't have a great grandfather," Jaxson said.

"Apparently I do." She drew in a deep breath before calling out again. "Marinda!"

"How big is this place? And are you sure she's here?" Jaxson asked.

Before Elsie could call out again, Harold appeared in front of her. "Are you trying to help him find her?"

"What?" She had no idea what he was going on about. She started to ask him to explain when he grabbed hold of her arm.

The world shimmered and reformed and they were inside a room with two comfortable armchairs in front of an empty fireplace. Marinda rose from one of the armchairs at their arrival. She threw herself at Jaxson, nearly knocking him over. "You're safe. I can't believe you're safe."

Chapter Twenty-Four

Elsie scanned the area, surprised at how ordinary every-thing looked. She turned to Harold. "Is this your home?" She could still hear the unprocessed magic, but it wasn't as loud.

"Yes. So don't go bringing any trouble here."

"Who were you talking about before?" Elsie asked. "The person trying to find Marinda."

"The Fae boy you were with. He's wandering the grounds looking for her. He's rather tenacious," Harold said.

"He's been ordered to find her. He made a promise to obey a dream weaver," Elsie said.

Harold glanced at Marinda. "I know. Your friend has been keeping me entertained with what you've been do-ing. It's nice to see one of my descendants actually has a backbone. I blame my wife's family for how weak many of them were. None of her family amounted to anything."

"Have you considered it was your fault for not being there to help raise your descendants?" Elsie tried not to let how annoyed she was by his comment enter her voice.

"Touch a nerve, did I?"

"I liked my grandfather. He was a nice man. And he mourned your death his entire life, regretting he never had the chance to know you." She glared at Harold when he shrugged. "Don't you feel even the slightest bit guilty about that?"

"At least he had the opportunity to live. His older brother didn't," Harold said.

"Older brother?" She'd always been told her grandfather had been an only child.

"I was looking after him while my wife was recovering from the birth of our youngest, your grandfather. He wouldn't sleep, so I lay down next to him. A dream weaver took him and I did everything possible to get him back, even becoming a dream weaver. It didn't help. So don't tell me I wasn't there for my family. I left for them," Harold stated.

"Sorry." She tried to think of something else to say, wishing she was part of the conversation between Marinda and Jaxson. They spoke quietly enough she only heard the occasional word. Anything had to be better than the conversation with Harold. She'd certainly made a mess of it. "I didn't know. Everyone believed grandad was an only child."

"We thought it best that way," Harold said. "How could we have explained all of this?" He made a sweeping gesture indicating the direction the constant noise came from.

"Doesn't it bother you?" Elsie asked.

"What in particular?" Harold asked.

She nodded in the direction of the unprocessed magic. "The noise. It sets my teeth on edge."

"You become slightly accustomed to it." He shrugged. "Either that or go insane. Although sometimes it's hard to tell which one you've achieved."

"I need to go home. Or…" Her voice trailed off. "Actually, I think I need to figure out a way to convince my mum to go somewhere else. Otherwise the dream weaver might make Caidon go after her if he can't find Marinda." She also needed to figure out a way to help Caidon escape from the dream weaver. She wasn't about to leave him there for the next decade. Not since she was the reason he'd failed to live up to his end of the bargain.

"You're not going to be able to remain in the human world. There's too much iron," Harold warned.

"Where am I meant to go?" Elsie demanded. It wasn't like she had anywhere else to stay.

"If you help process the magic, you may stay here for six days each month," Harold offered. "I don't need any more dream spinners turning up with their items that need processing. You might have noticed I already have far too many items that contain unprocessed magic."

"Sounds like you're the one getting the best out of that deal," Elsie said.

Harold shrugged. "Do you have another option?"

She thought of what the dream weaver had offered her. "Not one I like." Although she might be able to strike a deal with him to stay six days at his place in exchange for processing some of the items there. She certainly didn't want to increase the amount of unprocessed magic in any area by staying longer. She rubbed her temples. "How long does it take to get used to the noise?"

Harold shrugged again. "Dream weavers often have two places. One where they sleep and one where they store the items."

"Why not just process everything instead?"

Harold slowly shook his head. "You'll soon learn how impossible that is. Even more so when those who bring you items are from a location full of lost dreams."

"Isn't there anything that can help with the noise?" She wanted to press her hands over her ears, but that wouldn't do anything. It was more a sound she heard with her mind than with her ears.

"There's a circlet made from twenty drops of dream weaver magic. The trolls make them. No one dares store that much pure dream weaver magic in one place. The noise of it would be worse than ten times what's out there." He gestured in the direction of his towering piles of items. "So there's only one in existence. They say the one who had it made went insane and never had the chance to use it. His apprentice took it from him and she wears it to this day."

Plans started to fall into place. Elsie smiled. She might be able to get something the dream weaver wanted after all. Surely every dream weaver would want a circlet like that if it meant getting rid of the noise. "How many drops could you have in one location?"

Harold shrugged. "Possibly six. Seven would probably be too much. Even six might be too many."

"What are you planning?" Marinda moved closer, leaving Jaxson slumped in one of the armchairs.

Harold spun to face Jaxson, pointing a finger at him. "Don't you dare go to sleep. The dream weaver you were stolen from will find you."

Elsie took a vial of magic from her pocket and held it out to Jaxson. "This will help. Although it'll cause other problems."

Jaxson remained slumped in the chair, his hand shaking when he reached for the vial. "What is it?"

"Magic," Marinda said. "I can't wait to figure out how to use mine." She sent a daggered look towards Harold. "It's not like it would have taken a great deal of effort to tell me something of how to use it after all the questions I answered."

Harold ignored the look Marinda gave him, turning instead to Elsie. "You'd better explain all the side effects to the boy. You've probably got enough people after you without adding another wanting revenge for getting him into something when he didn't know what it was all about."

"I'd never blame Elsie. Not after what she went through to save me," Jaxson protested.

"You'd never be able to live for any length of time in the human world. Usually it's best to let everyone there think you died. You'd also have no one to help you start your life here in this realm, so there's a chance you'd not live long or end up the pet of some depraved Fae." Harold stopped in front of Jaxson, looking down at him. "Still willing to have magic?"

"What about my mum? I can't leave her thinking I died. Or leave her behind. She has no one else," Jaxson protested.

"Can't you bring her here too?" Marinda asked. "We have more magic. She could have some of her own."

Elsie wasn't sure if Caidon needed his magic back or if they could share it around, like Marinda suggested. That would only leave a single vial if they gave one to Jaxson's mum. "Can't I process dream weaver magic and sell it to earn money to support us here? I'm not about to dump my friends in some unknown world and expect them to fend for themselves. We're in this together."

Marinda stood shoulder to shoulder with Elsie. "All of us together. Like it always is."

Elsie smiled at Marinda before returning her attention to Harold. "See." She wasn't about to point out that it was usually just her and Marinda doing things together. He didn't need to know that.

"Do you even know how to draw magic out of objects?" Harold asked.

This time it was Elsie who shrugged. She wasn't about to let him see how worried she was about learning how to be a dream weaver and figuring out exactly what it meant to be one. "How hard can it be?"

Harold grabbed hold of her arm, pulling her away from Marinda. The world shimmered and reformed. He gestured towards a workbench similar to the one the dream weaver had in his tower. This one was in a small room with timber bookshelves along one wall crammed with items filled with unprocessed magic. "Go ahead. Show me how it's done. There are vials in the workbench drawer."

She took a few hesitant steps forward, glancing at the noisy shelves. "How are you meant to concentrate with all of this noise?"

"Are you giving up already?" Harold demanded.

"Of course I'm not. I just asked a question." She strode over to the workbench, taking a vial out of the drawer and putting it into place below the point of the angled mesh. Turning, she faced the shelves. "How many items will I need for a single drop?"

"Fill the mesh shelf," Harold ordered.

She started to take a step forward, then stopped. "Who gets the drop if I process it?"

"Process two and one is yours. Process one and only I end up with anything out of this exercise," Harold said.

She studied him, not sure if he was trying to trick her. "How long do I have to process the two drops?"

"Until you leave this room. Once you're finished in here, the opportunity is also over."

"What if I need to use the bathroom? Or have something to eat."

"You've been told the terms. Leave here and the opportunity is over," Harold stated.

She strode past him, her lips pressed firmly together against the words she wanted to speak. Alienating the one person who was helping, in his own fashion, wasn't a good way to start her life as a dream weaver. She gathered up an armful of items and returned to the workbench, where she put them on the mesh. She needed to bring three more armfuls over before it was full.

She stared at the workbench, trying to remember what the dream weaver had done. Raising her hands, she held them the same as he'd held his. She felt a drawing, tingling feeling in her palms. Frowning, she concentrated on it. What was she meant to do with it? How was she meant to pull the magic from the items? At the thought of pulling, the drawing sensation increased.

"You've seen this done before, haven't you?" Harold asked.

She glanced at him, seeing the surprise in his expression before he masked it. "You were expecting me to fail."

He shrugged, not giving her an answer.

Chapter Twenty-Five

Elsie's eyes narrowed and she returned her attention to the workbench, determined to form two drops of magic rather than the zero Harold had obviously expected her to gain. It was only when she thought of pulling the magic from the items that anything happened. A glimmer of light formed at the point of the mesh. Excitement raced through her and she focused harder.

The larger the drop of magic became, the greater the pressure in her head grew. It became a piercing headache and she gritted her teeth as she tried to ignore it. The magic formed slower and she fought to increase the speed, her mouth opening as she drew in a sharp breath from the pain radiating through her head.

"Not so simple, is it?" Harold asked.

She tried to ignore his smug words, pulling the magic from the items as quickly as she could. As the drop of magic fell into the vial, her head exploded with pain and she fell to her knees, breathing shallowly as she struggled not to pass out. She pressed her hands against the floor when the room spun around her, making her feel like she might throw up.

"I'm surprised you gained a single drop." Harold took a cork from the workbench drawer and pressed it into the opening of the vial before tucking it into his pocket.

She tried to speak. The pain made it impossible.

"Ready for me to take you back to my house?" Harold held out a hand to her.

She closed her eyes, shaking her head, remaining where she was on her knees.

"I don't have all day." He continued to hold out his hand.

Again she shook her head.

"You can't take another drop of magic from these items with the state you're in." He lowered his hand.

She drew in a shaky breath. "You didn't set a limit for how long I can stay in here."

Harold studied her a moment before laughing, the same deep, rolling sound as before. "Obviously a mistake on my part. I'll be back in an hour. Maybe you'll have had enough by then." He vanished.

Elsie lowered her head to the floor, resting her cheek against the cool timber floorboards. Was it safe to sleep now she was no longer a dream spinner? She had no idea, but couldn't remain awake a moment longer.

She woke to find Harold standing over her, his hands on his hips. She struggled to rise, her head aching and her body stiff. "How long was I asleep?"

"Four hours."

"Are Marinda and Jaxson okay?"

"No one can enter my house unless I allow it," Harold said.

She stood in front of him. "Why are you helping me? What do you want?"

"The same every dream weaver wants. To get rid of all the unprocessed magic around them. I want silence."

She met his gaze. "I want a circlet."

"You haven't put up with the noise for a day and already you want a means to silence it?"

"I don't want it for myself. I want to trade it for Caidon."

"You would do all this for a Fae you barely know?"

Images filled her mind. Ones of Caidon and all they'd been through together. Her lips curved into a smile as she recalled their kiss. "I do know him. He's loyal and willing to risk himself for others. I won't stop until I get him away from the dream weaver." Besides, it was her fault he had to serve the dream weaver for a decade.

"There's a stronger version of the dream weaver circlet. It takes forty drops of magic to make and not only does it silence the noise, but it doubles the amount of time you can stay in an area, hides you from dream spinners while you sleep and reduces the pain that drawing magic from items causes. You aren't the only one who'd be interested in owning a circlet."

"You said that having six drops in an area would be nearly impossible to put up with," Elsie said.

"The Trolls make the first version, then need another twenty drops of magic to turn it into the final version. If you can find a dream weaver willing to store five drops of magic at a time, I know of one I can trust to keep her end of the bargain so that all four of us will each have a dream weaver circlet."

"Who would get the first one?" Elsie asked.

"No one. We'd have the Trolls keep them until all four are made and then collect them at the same time. What do you think?"

"Can we trust the Trolls?"

Harold chuckled. "They wouldn't want to mess with a single dream weaver, let alone four of us. We'd make their nightmares come true."

"I'd need to generate forty drops of magic in total?" Elsie asked.

"Probably a few extra since the Trolls will want payment," Harold said. "What do you say? Granddaughter."

The word made anger fill her and she drew in a slow breath. "There was a time when you didn't appreciate the fact we're related."

"I expected you to be like Ron. Always demanding. Always complaining."

"I'm not like him." Nor did she want to be anything like him.

"So I've noticed. Your friend had a lot to say about you. And Ron. Everything she said about you was complimentary. Everything about Ron was anything but."

A smile reluctantly formed, the anger fading a little. "Yeah, Marinda doesn't like him at all."

"And you?"

She shrugged. It wasn't something she liked to think about. "He's my father."

"But do you like him?"

"What's that got to do with anything?"

"I guess I have my answer. Don't feel bad about it. There's nothing to say you have to like your parents if they're defective."

She felt like she should defend her father, yet she couldn't exactly think of anything good to say about him. "I need to take another drop of magic from these." She nodded towards the items still on the angled mesh.

"There's no need," Harold said. "You've proven you can do it."

"I want my drop of magic. Marinda and Jaxson will need something they can sell to help them afford to live in this world."

"They're not your responsibility. Haven't you realised that yet? This," he gestured towards the workbench, "is your responsibility. Not anything or anyone else."

"Why is it my responsibility? You make it sound like it's some kind of important mission."

"It is. The human world can't survive with all this unprocessed magic in it. Things go wrong. It needs us just like it needs the dream spinners. We do the world a service by siphoning off the pain of lost dreams. All that unprocessed magic left loose in the world would cause suffering, depression and even wars."

"Wars." Surely that couldn't be true. Maybe someone had lied to him.

"Wars. Haven't you realised yet that we can't lie?"

"We can tell a lie if we believe it to be true."

"I've seen the results of letting the magic remain in your world. It's our responsibility to keep the magic in this realm, not let it return. Nothing else is your responsibility. You made the choice to take it on, now you need to live with the responsibility."

She shrugged, not bothering to answer since she didn't have time to argue the point with him. Surely there was no reason why she couldn't look out for her friends and take care of the magic of lost dreams. Taking a deep breath, she tensed as she raised her hands, dreading the coming pain. Like before, she barely drew a drop of magic from the items before she collapsed on the floor, struggling to stay conscious. When she could finally speak, she looked up at him. "Does it get any better?"

"With time and practice you can bear the pain easier." Harold held out the corked vial to her.

Gritting her teeth against the pain, she pocketed it, struggling to rise to her feet. "Where will I store my magic for the circlet? Obviously I can't store it here with yours."

"I'll take you to the cottage where I first stayed when I came to this world. My old workbench is there. It's nothing fancy, but it will do until you can afford your own place and we're done with gaining the drops of magic needed for the circlets."

"What about my friends?"

"What about them?" Harold asked.

"I need to make sure they're safe first. Can they stay at the cottage too?"

"Why waste your time on them? They can't help you," Harold said. "Only cause problems. You have other responsibilities. Don't forget that."

"I'm not about to ditch my friends." She glared at him. "Is that the kind of loyalty I can expect from you if I agree to help?"

"That would be different. We'd both be contributing," Harold said.

"I'm not agreeing to anything that means I'd have to ditch my friends. Just keep that in mind," Elsie warned.

He held out his hand. "I'll take you back to them."

Elsie took his hand, the world shimmering and reforming the moment she did. Marinda threw herself at her as she arrived, knocking Harold's hand from her light grip. "He kept saying you were okay, but wouldn't take us to you so we could see for ourselves." Marinda sent a glare in Harold's direction.

He formed a pebble and held it out to Elsie. "You should be able to make your own, but so we're not left standing around waiting on you rather than getting on with things, use this one to take you home."

"What about to bring us back here?" Elsie took the pebble from him, also taking the second one he formed.

"I'll speak to the dream weaver I know while you're gone and you speak to the one you know before you return," Harold said.

"What if I can't figure out how to get to his place?" Elsie asked.

"You can't expect me to do everything for you."

"You can't expect me to know how to do everything the moment I become a dream weaver." She stood toe to toe with him, matching his glare with one of her own. "Did you instantly know how to be a dream weaver when you became one?"

"Do you expect me to recall something that happened that long ago?" Harold asked.

She met his gaze. "Yes. I do."

He laughed. "You might do well at this after all, not taking words as they appear to be intended. I apprenticed myself. That's what most dream weavers do. How else are we meant to learn how to use our abilities?"

"I will expect you to teach me as part of the deal to gain circlets," Elsie said. "No other payment needed for your teachings."

He inclined his head. "We'll discuss it in further detail once you've talked to the other dream weaver and I've talked to the one I can trust."

"I'll be back after I've talked to him, or if I can't find a way to travel to him." She slipped one of the pebbles into her pocket, keeping hold of the second one.

"We will see," Harold said.

Elsie turned to Marinda and Jaxson. "Ready to go home?" It struck her that home wasn't the last place she'd travelled from. She spun to face Harold. "Will the pebble take me back to where I came from? I don't want to take Jaxson to the dream weaver I rescued him from. That seems like a terrible idea."

"Picture the place you want to go," Harold said. "As a dream weaver, you can control the destination."

She glared at him. "You weren't going to tell me that?"

"I've already told you not to expect me to do all the work for you," Harold said. "You need to put some effort into learning about being a dream weaver."

Chapter Twenty-Six

Elsie drew in a slow, deep breath, making do with glaring at Harold rather than commenting angrily like she would have preferred. "I'll be back soon." She dropped the pebble onto the floor and grabbed Marinda and Jaxson's hands. She pictured her bedroom before she stepped on the pebble and the world shimmered and reformed.

"Elsie?"

She spun to face the doorway, surprised to find her mum looked a mess. "What happened?"

"You've been missing for two days. What do you mean, what happened?" Brenda demanded.

She stared at her mum. "Two days? Are you sure?"

"Where have you been? I returned to find your window smashed, blood on your bed and the two of you missing. Your handbag was still hanging on the door handle, untouched. Yet you weren't anywhere in sight. And who is that with you?" Brenda demanded.

Elsie glanced at Jaxson, once again reminded of how little he looked like himself. "It's Jaxson."

"What did you do to him?" Brenda took a step back.

Shock raced through Elsie. "You think I did this to him?"

"Well, I mean, how did you find him?" Brenda asked.

"You seriously think I hurt him," Elsie stated.

"No. It was the shock of seeing you. Of seeing all of you. The police…" Brenda's voice trailed off and she cleared her throat. "They think it was the same person. That someone is targeting our house." She turned to Marinda. "Your parents are staying with your mum's sister. You should give them a call and let them know you're safe."

Shaking her head, Marinda turned to Elsie. "I need to go home and pack. You should do the same. We'll meet back here. Do you have that vial in case Jaxson's mum wants to come too?"

Hoping that Caidon wouldn't need it, Elsie handed the vial over. "Grab a hat to wear. You probably don't want anyone recognising you." She didn't make the same suggestion to Jaxson. No one was going to recognise him. "And here." She gave the dream weaver magic to Marinda. "For you to sell to the magic collector."

Marinda took the vial, pocketing it. "Thanks."

Elsie hugged Marinda. "I'm not sure you should come back here."

Marinda returned the hug, squeezing Elsie tightly. "We'll use the portal Harold told me about and meet you back at his place."

Elsie nodded. "Okay."

Marinda and Jaxson slipped past Brenda, who remained in the doorway, having watched everything that was going on, a frown on her face.

"What is going on?" Brenda demanded once it was only the two of them. "Why are you talking about packing and leaving? Is someone targeting those in our house? We need to go to the police, if that's the case. Elsie, tell me what's wrong."

She stared at her mum, not sure how to explain everything to her. There was no way she'd believe a single word. Not without proof. Raising her hand, she studied her palm, trying to figure out how to form a pebble. Harold had said she'd be able to do it, but she didn't have a clue how. Nothing worked. Not imagining one and not thinking of pulling one to her like she'd pulled the magic towards her.

"Are you on drugs?" Brenda asked.

Elsie laughed, an abrupt, unexpected sound. "No. Not at all. Although you'll probably think I am."

"Why would I do that?"

"Because I don't have anything sane to tell you. Not if you want the truth and I'm afraid that's all I can give you these days."

"You're scaring me, Elsie."

"Dad told you, apparently. About dream weavers and spinners."

"You are on drugs," Brenda stated.

"No. I'm not." Elsie sighed. "It doesn't matter. You won't believe anything I have to say."

Brenda took out her phone. "I'll call someone for you to talk to-"

Elsie was across the room faster than she'd expected, taking the phone from her mum's hand. "No. You can't let anyone know I'm back. I can't stay."

"Are you in danger?"

She thought of everything that had happened and all that was still to come. "Yeah. More than likely."

"Then give me my phone and I'll call the police." Brenda held out her hand.

"They can't help me." She tossed the phone onto her bed, stepping in front of her mum when she tried to enter the bedroom. "Forget the phone. I want you to let Dad know I'm with his grandfather if either of you wants to see me. He should have a way to take you there if you're willing to go anywhere with him."

"Elsie-"

She interrupted her mum, knowing from her tone of voice that she was about to again suggest talking to someone. "I'm sorry I wasn't here when you came home and that I was gone so long. Time runs differently where I was. Keep that in mind if you visit."

"Elsie-"

Again she interrupted. "I'll come back and grab some gear. I don't have time to pack right now. So don't get rid of my stuff." She took out the pebble. She'd find another way back to Harold. Maybe the dream weaver would let Caidon have a few minutes to return her since she was trying to do something for him. In a way. She'd no sooner finished thinking about Caidon than he appeared in her room.

"Why did you have to return here?" He walked towards her. "You should have stayed away."

"Where did you come from? How did you get in here?" Brenda demanded.

Elsie slipped the pebble back into her pocket. "I need you to take me to him." She took hold of his hands. "I want to make a deal with him so you're not stuck serving him for the next decade."

He slid his arms around her waist, drawing her close and pressing her head against his shoulder. "Don't. I won't have you bound to him too. Just don't let me leave here with you. Your magic is strong enough that you'll be able to keep me here."

"I gave most of yours away. There's only a single vial left." She closed her eyes, ignoring her mum's demands as to what was going on.

"I don't need it. My magic will regenerate enough before I need that much again." His arms tightened around her. "You need to escape from me again. And take your mother with you. I don't want you to be forced to go to him because he has her."

She let herself enjoy being wrapped in his arms a moment longer before she drew back enough to meet his gaze. "I truly do have a way that might get you out of the bargain you made without taking your place instead."

"There's nothing he wants. I offered him all sorts of things when I was trying to rescue Autumn."

"A dream weaver circlet."

"What is that?"

"Apparently something every dream weaver wants."

Brenda grabbed hold of Elsie's arm, pulling her away from Caidon. "Don't ignore me, Elsie. Tell me what's going on."

"Ask Dad. Ask him to tell you about dream weavers and spinners. I have to go." Elsie pulled away from her mum, turning to Caidon. "Take me to him."

"He said to put you in one of the cages."

Brenda gasped. "Are you serious?"

"He'll want to hear my offer. Take me directly to him. Promise?"

"I promise." He held out a hand, smiling. "It doesn't completely override the promise I made to him, but it does make it easier to temporarily focus on what you've asked of me." He formed a leaf, crushing it in his hand.

The world shimmered and reformed and they were back in the room where they'd first met. Elsie lightly squeezed

Caidon's hand before she let it go. The dream weaver was only metres from her and from his expression, he wasn't impressed with Caidon having brought her to him. "Have you heard of a dream weaver circlet?"

"All dream weavers have. What has that to do with anything?" the dream weaver demanded. "You were meant to be put in one of the cages."

"How would you feel about being involved in creating four of the more powerful types?"

"What is the catch?" the dream weaver demanded.

"That Caidon and I owe you nothing and all those we took from you are no longer yours. You would also have to provide forty drops of magic, five at a time."

"And the time frame?"

"We'd begin soon. Trolls would hold on to the circlets until all of them were ready and we'd all collect them at the same time."

The dream weaver studied Elsie. "I'm still having to do a lot of the work. I'd expect more than just a circlet."

She wanted to protest. Didn't he want a dream weaver circlet? Surely something as powerful as that would be more than enough of a payment. "What else do you want?" She didn't manage to keep the sharpness out of her tone. But what could he expect by being greedy?

"I have five drops of magic. I want them brought to me. It'd be a waste leaving them where they are when I need so many," the dream weaver said.

"How difficult are they to collect and who has them?" Caidon asked.

Elsie sent him a grateful smile. She'd been about to agree to collect the drops of magic. "How long have they had them?"

"Several years."

She slowly shook her head. "And you think they haven't used them yet?" Was this a trick so she wouldn't be able to complete her part of the bargain?

"I know they haven't used them. They're still in the box I stored them in because I'd know if the magic seal had been broken," the dream weaver said.

"What if it's impossible to get them? What if she did everything reasonable to get them for you and it was an impossible task?" Caidon asked.

The dream weaver pointed a finger at him. "You will stay out of these negotiations."

"You will take back that order or you can miss out on a circlet," Elsie warned.

The dream weaver's lips twisted into a smile. "I have what you need more than you have what I need."

Chapter Twenty-Seven

Elsie mimicked the dream weaver's insincere smile. "I was told killing you would be easier."

The dream weaver's smile vanished. "Are you threatening me?"

"Were you threatening me?" Elsie asked.

The dream weaver's eyes narrowed. "You better not be mocking me."

"I'm not, and you better not be trying to change the subject. Take back your order. Part of the deal will include Caidon taking me to the places I need to go while fulfilling my part of the bargain. I'm only an apprentice when it comes to being a dream weaver."

"You may have Caidon's help during the time it takes to take back my magic, but I will have his help during the time it takes from then until the circlet is in my possession. I'll provide forty drops of magic, five at a time, and make no further claims on the two of you and the ones you took from me once you've provided me with my stolen magic and the most powerful type of a dream weaver circlet. All this needs to be done within the year." The dream weaver held her gaze for a moment. "Are you happy with these terms?"

She glanced at Caidon, who nodded slightly. "I'm happy to try and get your five drops of stolen magic as long as you also give me back the cushion from my couch."

"You would add that to the negotiations?" the dream weaver demanded.

She shrugged. "You added your lost magic to them."

"Fine," the dream weaver stated. "We have a deal."

"Where is your magic?" Caidon asked.

She placed a hand on Caidon's arm. "I need to carry news of our bargain to the other dream weavers first. Then we can go after the stolen magic."

"When you're ready to go after it, I'll take you there," the dream weaver said.

Elsie turned to Caidon. "Can you take me home first? I need to check on my mum."

Caidon took her hand, looking past her to the dream weaver. "What would you have me do?"

"Help the girl until she has my magic, or has failed at getting it back," the dream weaver said.

Elsie turned so she could meet the dream weaver's gaze. "My name is Elsie, not 'the girl'."

He held her gaze a moment before nodding and turning to Caidon. "Return with Elsie once an agreement has been reached with the other dream weavers and she's done what else needs doing regarding the matter."

"That better involve me being able to check my family is okay so I can concentrate on sorting out getting circlets," Elsie warned.

The dream weaver nodded again. "As long as this isn't a ruse to draw out the time."

"No, it isn't." Elsie stepped closer to Caidon, looking up at him. "Take me home."

He lowered his head so that his lips brushed her ear. "I wish I could." The scent of his magic filled the air and he crushed the leaf he formed, taking them to her bedroom.

She remained close to him. "What do you mean?"

"I'd like to take you to my home."

"I might have to take you up on that offer rather than draw dream spinners to me." She frowned. Had Harold been correct and they needed to take the magic out of the world so it didn't cause problems? If that was the case, she didn't want wars to start because she didn't feel like taking unwanted items from dream spinners.

"What is wrong?" Caidon asked.

She shook her head. "Something to worry about later. I need to find my mum." It didn't take her long to figure out her mum wasn't at home. When she tried ringing her phone, it went straight to the message bank. The same as it did for Jaxson, Marinda and her father. She slipped her phone into a pocket. "Where is everyone?" She checked the amount of time that had passed. Surely half a day wasn't so much time that Jaxson and Marinda were no longer in this world.

Caidon shrugged. "Did you want to visit their homes?"

Marinda's home was empty and, using the hidden key, Elsie let herself inside. She did a quick search of Marinda's bedroom. Her backpack was missing, along with some of her favourite clothes.

Jaxson's home was empty too. But there was no hidden key she could use to check what might be missing from his room. Not that she really would have known. She'd only been in his room a couple of times. Again she tried to call her parents. As before, the calls went straight to their message banks. She stared at the screen of her phone as the light dimmed. "Mum never goes anywhere that her phone doesn't get a signal. I can always get hold of her. Even if she's in a meeting she puts her phone on silent rather than turns it off."

"Did you want me to take you to Harold to see if Marinda and Jaxson have arrived there?" Caidon asked.

Elsie nodded, taking hold of his hand when he held it out. She smiled when he drew her close. Sliding her other arm around his waist, she leaned against him. "Can you teach me how to do this? How to form a pebble so I can travel to places using my magic."

He turned her hand, he held, palm up, placing a kiss against her palm before he spoke. "I draw my magic to this point and that allows me to form a leaf I can use to travel to places. I don't know if it's the same for dream weavers, but I know there are a few different methods amongst the Fae and each person has to figure out what works best for them."

She examined her palm, aware of Caidon's hand cradling hers. It took her a moment to find the magic coursing through her and pull it to her palm. Or at least pull enough of it to form a pebble. The one that formed was red. "Am I doing something wrong?"

"What do you mean? Didn't you want to form a pebble?"

"It's red."

"Yes."

"Should it be?"

He laughed softly. "They're different colours for different people. There's nothing wrong with yours."

"Really? I just assumed they were all black like Harold's." She slipped her pebble into a pocket of her jeans. "Do I use it the same way I use Harold's?"

"Picture where you want to go, then crush it. Travel should be easier for you since it works a little differently for dream weavers. And when you want to give someone a pebble to use, picture where you want it to take them as you're creating it."

"Okay. That doesn't sound too bad. How will I know if one I've made, to give to someone, was created properly?"

He grinned. "They will arrive at where you wanted them to go."

She returned his grin. "Okay. Fair enough." She thought of the black pebble Harold had given her. She'd keep it for an emergency. In case she ever struggled to create a pebble when she needed to get out of somewhere in a hurry. She'd also keep the one she'd made and test it when they weren't pressed for time. "I'm ready to return to Harold's."

Caidon formed a leaf, taking them straight to Harold's property. His arms tightened around her when she breathed in sharply.

It took a great deal of effort not to raise her hands to cover her ears against the noise. Reminding herself it wouldn't help, she spun to face the movement she could see in her peripheral vision.

Harold strode towards them. "Did you have to tell her to go to Ron? Now I'm stuck with him here." He grabbed hold of each of them by the shoulder and transported them to his place.

"What–" Elsie broke off when her mum hurried towards her, dragging her into her embrace. "Mum? What are you doing here?"

"You told me to come here." Brenda held her tight.

"Ah, not exactly. I told you to ask Dad what was going on." She returned her mum's hug, trying to pull away well before her mum was ready to let go.

"Couldn't convince her any other way." Ron turned to Harold. "If you give me two pebbles, I'll get out of your way and call in on you some other time. I mean, that message technique we were using wasn't working. Pebbles make more sense for when I need to see you."

"I'm sure I'll be as delighted to see you as every other time," Harold said dryly.

Startled by his words, Elsie initially thought Harold had figured out a way to lie until she thought over the words again. She grinned as Harold gave Ron two pebbles. One to take him home and the other to bring him back. She waited until Ron was gone before she spoke. "Nicely worded."

Harold laughed, his deep rolling one. "You'll get accustomed to how to reply in such a way. Now, do I take it you've made some sort of deal with the dream weaver?"

Elsie explained what had happened, slipping her hand in Caidon's when he moved close to her again. "So as soon as I've made sure everyone is okay, I'll head back to the dream weaver's place."

"As you can see, your mother is fine." Harold gestured towards Brenda. "She also doesn't appear to be as annoying as Ron."

"No one is as annoying as Ron," Brenda said.

Elsie spoke before her mum could get started on the list of how annoying her father was. "Has Marinda and Jaxson come here?"

"Not since all of you left," Harold said.

"If they turn up while I'm gone, can they wait here for me to return?" Elsie asked.

Harold nodded.

"And Mum can wait here too?" Elsie asked.

Harold shrugged. "Might as well. You're expecting me to let everyone else wait here."

"Do you have that last vial of magic on you?" Caidon asked.

Elsie nodded, taking it out of her pocket.

Caidon took it from her and held it out to Brenda. "If you plan to remain in this realm, you might want to consider having magic of your own."

Brenda took the vial. "Thank you."

"I'm sure Harold will tell you all the downsides to having magic." Elsie grinned at him.

"Someone has to make sure people make well-informed decisions," Harold said indignantly.

"Talking of decisions, what did the other dream weaver have to say?" Elsie asked.

"She's in," Harold said. "And the Trolls want a single drop of magic for each one they create. You can provide six drops each time since it was your idea."

Chapter Twenty-Eight

Elsie wanted to protest, but doubted she'd get a better deal. "I can manage that." She turned to Caidon, stumbling as she did so. "We need to return to the dream weaver's and get his magic for him."

"Elsie-"

The world shimmered and reformed before Elsie had the chance to hear her mum say more than her name. She looked around the bedroom they stood in, a large four-poster bed taking up most of the space, a wooden trunk at the foot of it. "Where are we?"

"My home." Caidon drew her forward. "You're tired. Rest before we return to the dream weaver's place. We can't afford to keep going like this. Or one of us will make a mistake due to how tired we are."

"Whose bed?"

"Mine. You can use it while I use one of the guest bedrooms. The other beds aren't as comfortable as this one." He pressed a finger against her lips when she started to protest. "I'll have the servants prepare food for us when we wake."

"I want to get this done. Don't you want to get out from under your promise?"

"Yes. Which is why we need sleep so we're not stumbling and failing when we go after his magic."

"Okay." She rested her head on his shoulder, forcing her impatience away. "I guess that makes sense."

"Then I'll see you in several hours." He shifted slightly so that she raised her head to look up at him, his lips meeting hers when she did.

Elsie clung to him, returning his kiss and protesting when he drew away.

"Time for sleep." He let go of her, taking several steps back. "I'll have a servant wait in the hallway for you so they can show you to the dining room when you wake."

She didn't want him to go, but he was right. They needed sleep. "Thank you for this. I'm so tired it's an effort to keep moving." The four hours she'd had earlier obviously hadn't been enough.

With a single nod and a brief smile, Caidon left the room, closing the door behind him.

She stared at the closed door for a moment before kicking off her sneakers and climbing into bed. The moment she relaxed against the pillow she was asleep, not struggling to fall asleep like she'd expected since it was a strange bed.

It was dark when she woke and she stumbled out of bed, trying to find the door. It opened before she reached it, a young man standing by it with a lantern. She slipped her feet into her sneakers before joining him in the doorway.

"Someone has gone to fetch Caidon. He'll meet you in the dining room if you'd like me to show you the way," the young man said.

She studied his ears as she followed him. He was human. "How did you end up in the realms of the Fae?"

He briefly touched his ears. "I was born here. Not all humans are new arrivals. Some of us are descended from those who've been here for centuries."

"Oh."

He smiled. "I'm not offended. I doubt you know much about this realm if you've only just arrived. I don't mind answering questions." He opened a door and stood back for her to enter.

She thanked him before she stepped into the dining room, smiling at Caidon, who rose from the table when she entered.

"Do you feel better?" Caidon came around the table and pulled out a chair for her.

"Yeah, but we need to get started on collecting the magic, not sit around eating." She dropped onto the seat he'd pulled out, the rest of her protests dying when she saw the food. "Well, maybe we can have a quick bite before we leave." She helped herself to the sweet pastries and the glass of juice that had been poured for her.

Caidon sat at the table opposite her. "We don't know how long it'll take to collect the magic so having something to eat first makes sense."

She could only nod, her mouth full and her stomach rumbling as it reminded her of how long it had been since she'd eaten. Swallowing the mouthful, she said, "We'll leave as soon as we've eaten."

"You didn't want to check back to see if Marinda or Jaxson have turned up at Harold's place yet?"

She was tempted to say yes, but doubted the dream weaver would be impressed if they drew the process out much longer. "I'll find out where they are after we've collected the magic."

Once they'd eaten, they readied themselves for the morning. Elsie put on a blouse Caidon had a servant give her after she'd had a wash in a wooden tub by the fire in his bedroom. Even though it was the last thing she wanted to do, she had the servant who waited in the hallway, take her to Caidon.

She held out a hand to him, taking two attempts to speak. Obviously, she wasn't really ready to go. "Take us back to the dream weaver."

Caidon took her hand and the room filled with the scent of his magic. They appeared in front of the dream weaver, who glared at them.

"About time you returned. Are you ready to fetch my magic now?" he demanded.

Elsie nodded, frowning when he handed her a drawing of a small, timber chest, decorative bands binding it. "What's this?"

"What you're looking for. It contains my magic and is about this big." The dream weaver held his hands twenty centimetres apart. "It's made of a dark timber and you won't be able to open it. The seal is still in place."

"Are you sure?" Elsie showed the picture to Caidon, her gaze remaining on the dream weaver.

"Of course I'm sure. I'd feel the seal break with how it's been bound."

"Why worry about this magic? You could make more instead of bothering with it," Elsie suggested.

"It's the principal. They don't deserve to keep them. It's my magic and they stole it from me. I want it back. Now, are you ready for me to transport you there?"

Elsie nodded, handing the paper back to the dream weaver. "We're ready." Although she would have preferred to argue his reason for wanting the magic. It seemed like a lot of effort for a few drops of magic, but what did she know about how this world worked?

The dream weaver tossed the drawing onto a side table and rested a hand on each of their shoulders. Once the world had finished reforming, he took a step back from them. "You can't use magic while you're inside. Return to me once you have the box." He vanished.

Elsie glared at the spot where he'd been. "He couldn't have told us that earlier?"

"There are probably a lot of things he hasn't told us." Caidon faced the manor house, which was set in immaculate gardens. "We should get closer so we can start working on a plan."

"There has to be at least three floors and what looks like an attic. How are we meant to find one little box in a place that big?" Elsie asked. "And during the middle of the morning when it's so bright we'll be easily seen."

"It probably has a basement too," Caidon said.

She turned her glare on him. "That doesn't help."

"It does because it's the most likely place to hide something of value. There'd be a single way in which would make it easier to guard," Caidon said.

"That doesn't help. How are we meant to get into a place so easily guarded?" Elsie asked. "Especially since we can't use magic."

"He said we can't use magic. He didn't say anything about dream weaver dust."

She frowned. "How will dust help? Unless it'll have them sneezing so hard they won't be able to do anything."

Caidon chuckled. "You know those tales you humans have about a sandman sending people to sleep?"

"Yes."

"That's you."

Her frown remained in place. "What is me?"

He lifted her hand, holding it palm up. "The sandman. You need to draw out your dream weaver dust."

"How do I do that?"

He ran the tips of his fingers across her palm. "I'm not a dream weaver. Do you need me to take you to Harold so you can ask him?"

She sighed heavily. "A pity the magic is in a special box, otherwise I'd have drawn five drops from items and given it to him. It'd have to be easier than this." And that was certainly saying something with what it felt like to harvest magic from the unwanted items dream spinners brought with them.

"You could have declined," Caidon suggested.

Chapter Twenty-Nine

Elsie met Caidon's gaze, looking into his vivid green eyes. "No, I couldn't. He was right. He has something I want more than I have something he wants. I'm not about to leave you with him for the next decade. Not since I was the one who caused you to be caught by your promise."

"You weren't at fault. You were doing the best to save your friend. And yourself. I don't blame you."

"Maybe you don't, but I do."

"Is that the only reason you're doing this? Because you think you owe me?" Caidon asked.

She grinned at him. "Nope. Not at all."

"What other reasons do you have?"

"I'm not about to wait a decade so I can spend time with you. I mean, I would wait if I had to, but I'm also going to do everything possible so we don't have to wait that long."

He pulled her close, his lips meeting hers as he held her tightly.

She returned his embrace, clinging to him as she kissed him back. Eventually, she drew away slightly. "We need to figure this out before someone opens the box and ruins our chances of getting you out of your promise."

He cupped her hand, holding it palm up. "Do you want me to take you to Harold, or do you think you can figure it out on your own?"

"I better try and figure it out on my own first. Harold keeps telling me he isn't going to do everything for me." She stared at her palm, trying several different things in an effort to make dream weaver dust. During the process, she created two pebbles she slipped into her pocket. About to give up, tired of trying to figure it out, dust began to form in her hand. Excitement raced through her and the dust stopped forming. "I had it. For a few seconds I had it."

"What did you do?"

"I don't know. I was tired and fed up with trying and then…" Her voice trailed off as she realised. "Tired. I put my exhaustion into the magic. Then it vanished when I was excited about figuring it out because I was no longer able to use my exhaustion to create the dust." She tested her theory, grinning when it worked, instantly stopping at her jubilation. She held out the handful of white, grainy dust. "I can do it." Her grin faded. "What do I do with it?"

Caidon laughed softly, glancing towards the manor house. "Toss it into their faces. Instant sleep."

"Cool. That's going to be so handy." She scanned the area where they stood. "It'd be a lot more handy if I had something to put it in."

"Look around for something when we're inside," Caidon said.

She studied the manor house ahead of them. "What's the plan?"

"Send everyone we come across to sleep." He led the way, his footsteps silent. After a moment, he stopped and turned to face Elsie. "You should be able to walk swiftly and silently. Focus on it. You're not exactly human anymore."

"I'm not what?" She slowly shook her head, certain she mustn't have heard him correctly.

"You have magic. You'd be considered Demi Fae."

"Does that make me part Fae?"

He shook his head. "I can answer your questions later. For now, we need to find the dream weaver's magic. And although it's nearly the middle of the day, it doesn't look like there are many people about. We should move while everything is quiet."

It took her a few attempts to be able to walk both swiftly and silently. She grinned. "Ninja skills. I wonder if Marinda and Jaxson have figured them out yet."

"We're approaching the manor house now. Remain silent," Caidon warned.

She scanned the area. "Is the place deserted? I can't see anyone."

"I don't know, but be careful in case it's a trap."

Her excitement over figuring out how to use some of her magic, faded. "We could be walking into a trap?"

"Anything is possible. But I hope we're not."

She didn't move as swiftly, reluctant to go any closer. Yet still she saw no one.

"Keep moving." Caidon kept his voice low.

She didn't argue that she was, because she had slowed down a lot, even if she was still moving. Reaching the front door, she scooped half the dust out of her hand so she had some in each. She held the dust ready, waiting for Caidon to open the door. The foyer was empty and she followed him inside. The moment she stepped into the house, she heard the cicada like noise of dream weaver magic, surprised she hadn't heard it sooner. They were definitely heading in the right direction.

They nearly stumbled on the first Fae they came across. Elsie automatically threw a handful of dust in his face while Caidon caught him before he hit the floor. They put him in a nearby room, closing the door before they continued on their way.

Elsie drew more dust into her hand, still not having seen something she could use to store it in. The next encounter was a Fae and a human. She threw a handful of dust at each, relieved she'd separated it when she'd had the chance.

Caidon caught the human and let the Fae fall to the floor. He put both of them in the closest room before leading the way into a kitchen. There were three humans, busy with various tasks, and they all turned to look in their direction. Elsie threw dust at two of them. The third tried to make a run for it. She generated more dust, throwing it at the human after Caidon tackled him to the floor. She drew more dust to her hands, not wanting to risk anyone escaping when she wasn't prepared.

A grin formed. She'd been worried over nothing. It was simple now she had dream weaver dust.

"The entrance to the basement is over here." Caidon straightened from putting the humans in a corner so they wouldn't be noticed immediately someone came into the room.

Elsie stopped in front of the basement entrance. "I know. I can hear the dream weaver magic down there. It gets louder the closer I am to it." She remained in front of the closed trapdoor. "What if there are more than two down there?"

"Send them all to sleep. One exit for them to guard also means only one exit for them to leave through." He opened the trapdoor.

She started to argue that it wasn't as easy as he made it sound. Approaching footsteps in the corridor outside the kitchen had her entering the basement, Caidon on her heels. She glanced around, ready to throw dust on anyone that might be in the basement. It was empty. At least of living things. The chests and cupboards, some of which were open, were a different matter altogether. They were filled with gold and silver coins along with various valuable looking items.

Caidon strode towards an open chest. "It can't be this simple." He took a decorative box out of the chest. "I'd expected guards down here."

Elsie joined him by the chest. "That is definitely the right one. I can hear the magic." The noise of it set her teeth on edge.

Caidon grabbed a cloth sack out of the chest that had contained the decorative box and slipped it inside once he'd tipped a handful of coins out of it. "We'll take it to the dream weaver and hope it's the one that belongs to him. Just because it contains dream weaver magic, it doesn't mean that it hasn't come from another. Although it looks like the drawing he showed us. Let's get out of here while it's still quiet."

They came out of the basement and collided with two Fae who were well armed. Elsie tried to throw dust at them, the two of them dodging out of the way. Fear rushed through her. Had the others been so easy to send to sleep because they were untrained?

The Fae closest to Caidon drew his sword and attacked. Caidon stumbled back, but not before the Fae's sword slashed across his arm, blood darkening his sleeve.

Elsie froze where she was, her gaze fixed on the blood darkening his sleeve. She was back there again, blood everywhere, frozen in place as the blood continued to flow. Her surroundings faded, only the blood visible.

"Throw dust on them," Caidon ordered. He ducked and weaved, both the Fae now attacking him. "Elsie! Please."

The frantic sound of his voice snapped her out enough that she automatically threw a handful of dust at the closest Fae. He collapsed onto the floor, instantly asleep. She tried not to pay attention to the blood on Caidon's sleeve, but it felt like it was all she could see. Feeling light headed, she swayed on her feet. Her heart raced and her mouth remained open, no sounds escaping. There was too much blood, some of it dripping onto the floor.

"The other one, Elsie. The other one now." Caidon took the sword from the sleeping Fae, blocking an attack from the other one.

She tried to make herself move. She remained where she was, the handful of dust clutched in her hand, her heart racing as she tried to block out the sight of the blood splattered across the floor.

"Elsie! Please," Caidon called out.

His pleas had her casting the second handful of dust. Caidon tackled the other Fae. It was too late for her to stop. Dust settled on both of them and they crashed to the floor. She stumbled forward to kneel at Caidon's side, shaking him, the pound of her heart loud in her ears. He didn't wake. Her hands were shaky and she removed the shirt of the Fae who was next to him so she could wrap it around

Caidon's arm and hide the blood. She felt a little better once she could no longer see it, her back to the splatter on the floor.

She shook him again. He remained asleep. Hoping the pebbles would work since they were made by dream weaver and not Fae magic, she took one out of her pocket and held onto Caidon's hand and the bag the box was in. She stepped on the pebble. Nothing happened. It remained intact. She tried all the pebbles in her pockets. Not a single one worked. Returning them to her pockets, she tried to drag Caidon towards the exit. She didn't manage to take him far. She wasn't strong enough. Although she did feel stronger than she usually was.

Looking between Caidon and the exit, she nearly groaned at the distance she had to move him. And that was only the exit of the kitchen. She had to get him through the rest of the manor house. Her attention was caught by a window and she peered out it at the gardens behind the house. She wasn't sure if she could get Caidon out the window, but it had to be easier than trying to drag him through the house.

Returning to his body, she caught sight of the blood on the floor. Bright red splatters that had her freezing in place. They remained the same, not growing in size and not slowly covering the floor like they did in her nightmares. She drew in a shaky breath, trying to make herself move. She couldn't stand here all day. What if someone entered the kitchen? Another shaky breath had her stumbling forward.

She dragged and pulled Caidon over to the window, desperately trying not to see the blood. Somehow her luck held and no one walked in on her as she manoeuvred him into place, dragging him up on a chair she'd placed under the window. But that was as far as she could get him. Frustration had her breathing out heavily, giving her something to focus on other than the blood. She tried to pull him up to the window. He was too heavy for her.

Chapter Thirty

The sound of approaching footsteps had Elsie straighten-
ing and calling dust to her hand. A female Fae had barely
stepped into the kitchen when the dust was settling over
her and she was dropping to the floor. Elsie stood where
she was by the window with Caidon, breathing fast from
the encounter. There was no way she could get Caidon
outside. She didn't have the strength and they couldn't
remain here until he woke because too many would wake
before him. She tried to shake him awake. It didn't help.

She leaned in close, whispering in his ear for fear someone might hear her. "Please wake up, Caidon."

At her words, he blinked groggily up at her. "What
happened?" His words were slurred.

She was surprised that something as simple as asking
him to wake had worked. "We have to get out of here." She
grabbed hold of the bag containing the chest. "Quickly.
We're going out the window." She climbed through first,
glad to leave the bloody scene behind.

Caidon climbed out after her, stumbling and landing sprawled across the ground.

She winced at the impact. Obviously the words hadn't completely woken him from the sleep the dust had put him in.

He waved her help away, finally getting to his feet. "How long was I asleep?"

"Not long." Although it had felt like an eternity to her. She closed the window, taking the box with her. When Caidon followed her through the garden, stumbling and staggering, she tried to steady him.

Again he brushed her away. "I'm too heavy for you."

"We have to get far enough away from here that we can use a pebble to escape." She grabbed hold of his arm when he stumbled, her stomach turning when she realised she touched the blood-soaked sleeve. She quickly let go, stepping back. Then she found herself rushing forward to prevent him from falling, trying not to think of the blood. There was a roaring sound in her ears and she breathed shallowly in an effort to remain conscious.

"I'm sorry they cut me." He glanced at his covered sleeve before he pulled away from her again. He took hold of her hand, drawing her with him as he stumbled and staggered his way to the edge of the gardens.

The moment the two of them were past the grounds, Elsie drew a single pebble out of her pocket. Before she could use it, someone entered the gardens to point at her, yelling. She couldn't make out what they were saying, but was fairly certain it wasn't a greeting. Dropping the pebble on the ground, she tried not to think about the Fae that ran towards them, drawing a sword. She doubted she'd survive seeing any more blood today. She was barely keeping it together. After making sure she was securely holding onto the bag containing the box, she grabbed hold of Caidon's hand. She stomped on the pebble as the Fae came within arm's reach.

The world shimmered and reformed around them. She smiled when she realised how close she'd brought them to the dream weaver's front door. Only a couple of steps away. She'd finally done something on her first attempt. She took the last couple of steps and leaned against the wall as she reached for the door, Caidon stumbling after her.

The door was wrenched open before she could attempt to open it herself. The dream weaver looked down at her. "You took an unnecessarily long amount of time to return this to me."

Elsie handed over the box, not saying a word. It wasn't like she could disagree. They'd taken time to sleep and eat before coming back to him last time.

The dream weaver placed his hand on the lid of the box and it popped open. Inside, on a bed of velvet, were five vials containing dream weaver magic. "This was exactly what I wanted. No one can have my magic without my permission." He closed the lid again. "You can use these to help create a circlet. You can take them to the Trolls for me." He held the box out to her again.

Relief rushed through her. They were done. She tried not to think about the blood as she took the box from him, not about to point out that she'd taken magic from him without his permission. "I don't know how to travel to the Trolls."

"You don't expect me to do everything for you, do you?" the dream weaver demanded.

His words reminded her of Harold, which made her smile. She slid an arm around Caidon's waist. "We'll see that this is delivered and then Caidon can come back to serve out his time with you while we wait for the circlets to be made."

"There's no need for you to take Caidon with you," the dream weaver stated.

Her arm tightened around Caidon's waist. "Our task isn't done yet. I'll bring him back when it is." She used a pebble to return to Harold's, still grinning. The dream weaver was likely to be annoyed over her ignoring his orders and treating them more like a suggestion. But she didn't care. Who knew how long it'd take to have the circlets made. She wanted to spend every last second possible with Caidon before he had to spend his time serving the dream weaver. And she needed to see that his wound was cleaned. What if the dream weaver didn't get it taken care of and he ended up with an infection? Someone else would have to clean it. She wouldn't be able to manage.

She turned to meet Caidon's gaze, leaning in for a kiss when he smiled down at her. Somehow they'd both survived and completed the near impossible task the dream weaver had set them. Now they only had to take magic to the Trolls and wait for the circlets to be made. Then Caidon would be free of the dream weaver. They all would be free.

* * *

Elsie stood beside Harold, the other two dream weavers on his left and Caidon standing behind them. No one spoke as they waited for the Trolls to bring out the circlets. Elsie kept glancing at Caidon. It was the first time she'd seen him since they'd given the first lot of vials of magic to the Trolls. She wanted to take his shirt off and check to see if the wound had healed properly. Although it should have, since it had been three months. Three very long months without him. Not even his sister had been allowed to see him.

Caidon caught her gaze, smiling at her before he returned his attention to the four Trolls coming towards them, each carrying a circlet.

The narrow circles were made of silver, the front of them meeting in a point that contained a dream weaver pebble. The one for Harold's friend had a green pebble, Harold's was black, hers was red and the other dream weaver's was a dark grey. Elsie took the circlet that was held out to her, placing it on top of her head where it sat like a simple crown. The low, dull ache that had formed earlier, when she'd been working on processing dream weaver magic, instantly vanished.

Harold's friend thanked them before she formed a pebble and used it to leave. Harold started to do the same. Elsie grabbed hold of his hand before he could release the pebble. "Do we get to keep staying at your old cottage?" It was rather crowded with her mum, Marinda, Jaxson and his mum, but at least it was somewhere safe and dry for them to stay.

"You're my apprentice, aren't you?" Harold asked.

She shrugged. "Of a fashion." She wasn't about to let him trick her into anything.

"Then you must stay somewhere and I'm not having the lot of you under my feet." Harold drew out of her grip. "I'll expect you in the morning for your next lesson." He dropped the pebble on the ground and stepped on it, vanishing.

Elsie couldn't resist a grin. Harold didn't dislike all of those staying at her cottage. She was pretty sure he more than liked Jaxson's mum and he was even civil to her mum, particularly when they commiserated with each other about Ron. He wasn't that keen on Jaxson, but he did like Marinda since she didn't mind telling him everything that was going on in their lives. And he also didn't mind

Autumn, who was regularly at their place, visiting with Jaxson and these days looking very pregnant.

The dream weaver turned to Elsie the moment the Trolls had gone, leaving only the three of them in the area. "You met your end of the bargain. The lad is yours and you owe me nothing. The cushion is yours to collect."

Elsie nodded, not sure what to say in the situation. As soon as the dream weaver vanished, she turned to Caidon, grinning. "Did you hear that? You're mine."

He chuckled softly, drawing her into his arms. "Fae are never the pets of humans. It's always the other way around."

She grinned up at him. "But I'm not human. Didn't you already tell me that?" She tightened her arms around him. "I'm a dream weaver." And with the help of the circlet, she'd be able to process even more magic from lost dreams, ensuring that the human world would become less chaotic. Or at least the part of the world her dream spinners came from. She'd been able to track down where some of them came from, and those ones certainly needed the help of a dream weaver in their various locations.

"You ready to come home with me?" Caidon asked.

She savoured the words, nodding. "I like the sound of that." She'd missed him these past few months. Only exchanging letters each time she'd collected drops of magic to take to the Trolls, Caidon having convinced one of the dream weaver's servants to give her his letters. "We have a lot to catch up on." She grinned. "And plenty of time in which to do it."

The peppery citrus scent filled the air as Caidon crushed the leaf he'd formed, one arm staying around her. The world shimmered and reformed and they were out the front of his house. "Welcome home."

She rested her head against his shoulder. "I was already home." She tightened her arms around him, smiling when he tightened his arms around her.

"Being with you feels like home to me too." His lips met hers when she rose on the tips of her toes. Eventually, he drew back, staring down at her. "And I couldn't imagine being anywhere else."

She met his gaze, staring into his vivid green eyes. It was hard to believe it was only a few months ago that she'd woken to see his eyes staring down at her. "I couldn't imagine being anywhere else either. Or being anything else." Again she rose onto the tips of her toes, pressing her lips against his when he lowered his head to meet her. It hadn't taken her long to realise she was meant to be a dream weaver. Or a sandman, as she'd needed to be a few times when dream spinners had woken or brought people with them. A typical job like what her mum had once held wasn't for her.

Nor was she like the dream weaver who'd imprisoned Jaxson. She didn't need to take magic from the unwanted. She took enough other magic from the world. It would keep her areas safe. She'd already noticed the difference she'd made in the short time she'd been a dream weaver.

She drew back from Caidon, once more meeting his gaze. "Meeting you has been a dream come true." And she should know. She was a dream weaver and had the power to alter people's dreams even if she couldn't make them come true. That apparently could happen if she lived long enough and became powerful enough. Not that she knew what she'd do with an ability like that. Make the dreams of the unwanted come true? Who knew. Maybe one day she'd find out.

She smiled up at Caidon when his arms tightened around her and he drew her in for a kiss. Who knew what her future held. But whatever it was, she was looking forward to finding out.

Free Ebook

Subscribe to Avril's newsletter and receive a free ebook. This ebook is exclusive to those on her mailing list. To find out more about this offer visit:

https://www.avrilsabine.com/free-ebook

*

We value your privacy and will not sell, rent, exchange or loan your email address to third parties. Your information is confidential and you are under no obligation to remain on the mailing list and can unsubscribe at any time.

Acknowledgements

A special thanks to the usual crew, particularly since there were added difficulties to the way we normally do things due to the current world situation.

To The Reader

If you enjoyed this book, why not consider leaving a review to help other readers discover it too? Reader engagement is one of the few ways that lets an author know readers want more books in a particular series or genre. So leave a review and tell friends, not only about this book but also about other ones you've enjoyed, so you can continue to enjoy books by your favourite authors for years to come.

Dreams are meant to be lived,

Avril.

About The Author

Avril is an Australian author who lives with her family on acreage in South East Queensland. She writes mostly young adult and children's speculative fiction, but has been known to dabble in other genres. You can find more information about her at https://www.avrilsabine.com where you can also subscribe to her newsletter to be kept informed about new releases, current projects, blog posts and exclusive news.

Titles By Avril Sabine

Stories about strong characters and characters who

discover their strengths.

Series

**Assassins Of The Dead- Young Adult Fanta-
sy/Paranormal**

Book 1: Dark Blade
Book 2: Dragon Touched
Book 3: Society Against Vampires
Book 4: King's Request
Book 5: Duke's Courier

**Dragon Blood- Young Adult Urban Fantasy
(with elements of romance)**

(5 book series)
Book 1: Pliethin
Book 2: Wyvern
Book 3: Surety
Book 4: Knight
Book 5: Mage

Dragon Mage- Young Adult Urban Fantasy (with elements of romance)

(Series two of Dragon Blood series)
Book 1: Promise
Book 2: Pact

Dragon Blood Chronicles- Young Adult Urban Fantasy (with elements of romance)

(Companion stand alone series to Dragon Blood)
Book 1: Oath
Book 2: Betrayed

Guardians Of The Round Table- Young Adult Fantasy LitRPG

(Co-written with Storm and Rhys Petersen)
Book 1: Dexterity Fail
Book 2: Goblin Boots
Book 3: Singed Feathers
Book 4: Frog Mage
Book 5: Crystal Mine
Book 6: Cursed Harp
Book 7: Treasure Seeker

Rosie's Rangers- Young Adult Western Steampunk

(6 book series)
Book 1: Justice
Book 2: Vengeance
Book 3: Treachery
Book 4: Accused
Book 5: Wanted
Book 6: Corruption

Mark Of Kings- Children's Fantasy

(Upper middle grade/preteen)
(4 book series)
Book 1: The Arena

Book 2: The Island

Book 3: The Assassin

Book 4: The King

Stand Alone Series

Demon Hunters– Young Adult Urban Fantasy/Horror (with elements of romance)

Book 1: Blood Sacrifice

Book 2: Retribution

Book 3: Tainted

Book 4: Premonition

Book 5: Cursed

Book 6: Feud

Book 7: Extrication

Plea Of The Damned– Young Adult Urban Fantasy/Paranormal

(6 book series)

Book 1: Forgive Me Lucy

Book 2: Forgive Me Aiden

Book 3: Forgive Me Jena

Book 4: Forgive Me Kobe

Book 5: Forgive Me Marti

Book 6: Forgive Me Dawson

Realms Of The Fae- Young Adult Urban Fantasy (with elements of romance)

The Sword (short story in Like A Girl Anthology)

Call Forth The Wild Hunt (Short story in Summer Solstice Shenanigans Anthology)

Heart Of Stone

Book 1: A Debt Owed

Book 2: Marked By The Hunt

Book 3: The Magic Collector

Book 4: An Unexpected Betrayal

Book 5: Imprisoned By Iron

Book 6: Woven From Dreams

Fairytales Retold (Short Stories)

Snow-White And Rose-Red

The Twelve Brothers

The Light Princess

Beauty And The Beast

Sleeping Beauty

Aschenputtel
The Golden Bird
The Frog Prince
The Death Of Koshchei The Deathless

Myths And Legends Retold (Short Stories)

Ion, Son Of Apollo
Sir Gawain And The Maid With The Narrow Sleeves
Princess Ilse, The Giant's Daughter

Young Adult Novels

Young Adult Fantasy (with elements of romance)

Elf Sight
Earth Bound

Young Adult Urban Fantasy

Stone Warrior (with elements of romance)
The Jungle Inside

Young Adult Contemporary (with elements of romance)

Through Your Eyes
The Ugly Stepsister
Perfect Little Princess

Young Adult Contemporary/Paranormal

Whispers In The Dark (with elements of romance)
Over Too Soon (with elements of romance)

Young Adult Sci-Fi

Experiment X-One-Six (Urban Sci-Fi/Superheroes)
An Endless Dawn (Post Apocalyptic Sci-Fi)

Children's Books

Dragon Lord (Preteen/early teens) (Fantasy)

The Irish Wizard (Upper middle grade) (Urban Fantasy)

Short Stories

Urban Fantasy

Eternally Late
Dealings With Joe
Glimpses (short story in That Moment When Anthology)

Contemporary

The Brat Next Door

Fantasy LitRPG

(Set in the same world as Guardians Of The Round Table Series)
Tales Of Inadon 1: The Disc (Co-written with Storm and Rhys Petersen) (short story in Game On! Anthology)

Post Apocalyptic Sci-Fi

Compulsive Directive

Nonfiction

A Year Of Weekly Writing Exercises (Creative Writing)
Cooking For Families With Allergies (Cooking)
(Co-written with Storm Petersen)
Tell Me A Story, Grandma (Memoir)

Online Course

Overview Of Independently Publishing A Book

For the most up to date details on available titles visit:
www.avrilsabine.com/books/bibliography

Realms Of The Fae Series

To learn more about this series visit:
https://www.avrilsabine.com/series/rotf

Books available in the Realms Of The Fae series
The Sword (short story in Like A Girl Anthology)
Call Forth The Wild Hunt (Short story in Summer Solstice Shenanigans Anthology)
Heart Of Stone (Prequel)
Book 1: A Debt Owed
Book 2: Marked By The Hunt
Book 3: The Magic Collector
Book 4: An Unexpected Betrayal
Book 5: Imprisoned By Iron
Book 6: Woven From Dreams

Disclaimer

This is a work of fiction. Names, characters, businesses, places, events and incidents are either the products of the author's imagination or used in a fictitious manner. Any resemblance to actual persons, living or dead, or actual events is purely coincidental. The opinions expressed or beliefs held are those of the characters and should not be assumed to be the opinions or beliefs of the author.

www.ingramcontent.com/pod-product-compliance
Lightning Source LLC
Chambersburg PA
CBHW050806190726
48285CB00005B/1809